T

The Tangle Box
by Dave Kavanagh

First published in Ireland in 2021
by Chaffinch Press

ISBN: 978-1-8384025-4-9

For Ber, Shaun, Adam and Rou

A memory

Behind me is the yard. The barn roof needs painting; it was red once, but now it's peeling back to metal grey. Streaks of orange rust run down the walls like blood. The wind breaks against it and a loose gutter sounds like a discordant bell.

In front of me, beyond the rank seeding grass and the hawthorn ditch, the sea looms grey and bruised — even from this distance I can see whitecaps, and smell the salt blowing inland. Gulls cry, hanging on threads of air, then dart forward as the breeze takes them.

The grass bends towards me, trembling and quaking like the ocean, waves forming as the wind whips through it. The meadow is no longer lush. It's overgrown, too bitter now to make good hay. Da should have cut it weeks ago, but he's too sad to mow, too sad to stand, or even speak. He spends his day sitting on the harbour wall, staring out to sea.

There's a storm coming, the prickly feel of it like salt rubbed into my skin. My arms and fingers are itchy from it. The storm light paints the field from dark, solemn green to vibrant yellow. Bands move across the grass like a knife smearing butter over warm toast.

I turn towards the farmyard. A rooster clucks and stalks four hens, his beady eyes dark and dangerous. A sudden sunburst freezes him in place, his luminous plumage of green, red and orange vibrating against the background of grey dust.

Jess is not running in front of me; instead she is beside me, hunched low, nervously herding ducks back towards the hen-house.

The barn rattles. On the feather-house roof, sparrows argue in loud, fractious voices; they hover, half-flying, then the wind buffets them back down. The trailing ends of the honeysuckle they perch on tremble, then lift in a tangle of flailing tendrils as the wind catches them.

The dark clouds loom — great pregnant bellies of black and purple, their edges glistening white, too bright to look at. Shafts of light escape in bursts and probe the stone of the yard like needles; grey cobbles shine iridescent and then as quickly fade back to muted tones as the sun moves back into the clouds.

A shadow dashes across the yard — the cat, Gráinneog, her back arched. She darts to the machine shed, her hiss escaping like air from a ball. She turns and glares at me, her back bristling.

I'm aware of other sounds. In the barn, the five pigs squeal as though poked by a stick, skittering as they rush about the pen, and then fall silent as they settle.

The first drop of rain falls, and pockmarks erupt in the dust — more come, drops so big they bounce off my arms, warm and soft as blood.

The sparrows have gone quiet.

The trees behind the house move in the wind, the sound of branches clashing and leaves waving inaudible in the storm's tumult.

Another sound comes, a screaming voice. I run. My hair is soaking — water streams down into my eyes, wetting my lips; I squint through it. I hear a second scream — cut off. My ears are full of the silence that follows, my arms flailing as I run.

At the house I stop, hesitate at the door: The Lady in the Glass is shimmering, the rain streaming down her etched form.

There's thunder — a long low boom like an angry tide breaking on rocks. The wind changes direction and carries other sounds to me — a dog barking, the wind, rain lashing off the barn, sounds merging.

My hand lifts and pushes the door inwards. The wind catches it and slams it back against the inner wall — there is a twanging aftershock as it vibrates.

A strangled animal sound erupts from my lips. The floor is wet, soaked from the rain that blows in behind me. The wind enters, lifting curtains and rising smoke from the fireplace. Rain beats on the roof, large drops racing each other down the window glass.

I pass through the front room. The screaming has stopped — now there is a terrifying silence. I hesitate at the entry to the kitchen; there's a smell, something vile like rotten meat or vomit, and my nose wrinkles in disgust.

I jump across the black step and land on the linoleum of the kitchen floor, my impetus carrying me forward on the wetness, not rain, the rain cannot have entered this far. It's something else.

Blood.

*

The memory ends there and I can't see what lies beyond it.

The beginning

This is where it starts. I'm a stranger in a dimly lit room, staring into a mirror. In the reflection I see three white kitchen units hanging on a bare wall and, closer in, a breakfast bar strewn with the things I abandon there — yesterday's newspaper, folded over, the crossword complete. A fruit bowl, filled not with fruit but a car key, two bills, the stub of a cinema ticket and a hospital appointment card.

I move and the perspective swings to a bed folded into a wall, springs exposed, a white sliding door, and a coffee table with four books stacked on it: Capote, Melville, Atwood, Connolly.

I adjust my focus and regard the man staring back at me. His eyes are deep brown, almost black and set in hollows — jaded, Caroline would have called them — the eyes of a man older than my forty-five years. My hair is dark, still damp from the shower but it will dry as I walk to the station. My face is thin, just short of gaunt, and my skin pale from lack of sun.

My greying beard hides the damage to my jaw. My index finger traces a line from the softness beneath my chin to the edge of my left cheek, halting where the scar is visible, an angry red exclamation mark. When I press my finger hard against it, it fades, then reappears once I remove the pressure.

I'm wearing my best clothes. A white shirt, open

at the neck (I don't own a tie). It's close fitting and tucked into faded blue jeans that fitted me once but are now two sizes too big. My belt looks wide on my narrow waist, and the buckle, bright when it was new, is now black and tarnished. I wear the only pair of shoes I own, of a soft brown leather, scuffed, but comfortable.

I turn and face the room. The estate agent advertised it as a studio. It is rectangular, but for a sectioned-off corner that breaks the symmetry. There, two drywall slabs conceal a toilet and a shower stall, all arranged in a space not much larger than an airing cupboard.

I've lived here for seventeen weeks, but it is not my home — it is a way station. I chose it because it suited my needs; it's inexpensive and allows me access to public transport.

The studio is tucked into the rear of the building, far from the front entrance which means it is private.

The only window faces out over a park where grass and trees are visible through black railings. When I arrived in April, the birds woke me each morning with their busyness. Now they've quietened, or I've become accustomed to them.

The people who come to the park arrive in shifts. Old men are the first, men who no longer work but still rise early, driven by habit or the need to do something; in the afternoon it is young mothers pushing prams or trailing young children. The evening group are loud and raucous, teenage boys, prowling like slouched predators, or girls, flocking like exotic birds, loud and bright. On weekends, I sit and watch them as they pass; I wonder at their sameness and the wonderful ordinariness of their lives.

In the in-between times, the late mornings and the afternoons, the park is empty.

I check my watch, it's 8.15 am. My jacket hangs by the door. I put it on, and then I take the crutch. I will walk the last stretch, so I will need it.

*

They subdivided the original house into four apartments and the studio I rent. It sits on a rise. I exit through the one-way door at the back of the building and pause. In front of me the sea shimmers, reflecting the washed-out blueness of a late August sky. In the near distance is the island, the smooth curved greens of the links at its centre, and at its edge, the bright whiteness of sand that sits like a bright carcanet above the tide line. The space between is rough grass, bleaching to an autumnal gold; it sways in the breeze, mimicking the sea. I breathe in the smell, mud and salt, and it overpowers the tang of the city behind me.

I turn and walk along the path at the side of the building, passing the car I have used only once in the previous month.

On the street that fronts the building, the daily parade of commuters is moving towards the station: a man in a light overcoat, head down, briefcase in hand; a woman in sensible red shoes, rushing by; a boy cycling past, whistling. I join them, my crutch scuffing the sunlit pavement.

The weight of the day descends. I feel the letter tucked into the front pocket of my jeans, its sharp edges digging into the skin between my hip and pelvis, where angry purple scars line the hollow.

*

At the station, people stand waiting, some chatting in groups, others alone or holding takeout coffee cups, avoiding eye contact. A girl wears earphones, dancing in place, her face distant as though the music transports her to somewhere less mundane. I move along the platform, away from the tinny repetitive beat.

People see the crutch, not me; they move aside and give me room to pass and I find a clear section of wall to lean against. My leg is already aching and I regret not driving into the city.

An electronic noticeboard announces the train times in red letters. My train will come in seven minutes. I withdraw the letter. The crease lines along the folds are darkening, I've read it so many times I can recite the words by heart, but I unfold it and read it again.

A letter

Dear Danny,

First, a big truth — I am alive. I know it's been cruel to keep that from you. There is a second big truth, but that you must discover yourself.

On the day I left, Da helped me to get away. He told me later that you remembered nothing, that you only knew that I had left, and Ma too. He said you were better off not knowing what happened, that it would be too painful, and I agreed with him.

I was wrong. I know that now. You deserve the truth, but you need to find it yourself. It is there, Danny, wrapped in memories you were always too innocent to allow.

I have enclosed Cathryn Ryan's card. She is a woman I trust. She can help you, Danny — she is expecting your call and I pray that you will make it.

I know this will be difficult, but please try to understand. I love you, I never stopped loving you. In my memory we are close, we are survivors. We are warriors, do you remember?

These are the memories that sustain me and I'm terrified of losing them.

Love, Maria.

The city

The tannoy announces my train; I fold the letter and replace it in my jeans pocket. The crowd surges forward and I hang back, avoiding those who shoulder their way through. I'm in no rush. There will be no empty seats on the morning train, there never are, but the journey is short. I board and as the train moves forward, I grab for a pole and lean back against it. I close my eyes and think of Maria, my beautiful, damaged sister.

*

When I was fourteen years old, my mother and sister disappeared. On that day, I woke beneath a roof of grey asbestos sheeting. The room was cold. Maria was awake in the bed across from me, her back turned away, a book open on her pillow, and her dark hair tucked tight against her shoulder. Below, I could hear sounds, pots being placed on a stove, footsteps shuffling across flagstones. Voices from a radio, a weather report — there would be a storm later that day.

The light filtering through the Perspex skylight was bright; it painted a skewed rectangle on the bare boards.

I got up and stood beneath it, the boards under my feet rough and chill. Peering through the corrugations I saw, in the foreground, the feather-house and the machine shed, and beyond them, the barn. Da was there, working the block and tackle, oiling the chains, preparing for the slaughter.

*

The train screeches as it approaches the station, the scene beyond the window becomes distinct — smudged house gables, power lines, blue and red graffiti on a derelict redbrick warehouse. The train stops with a jolt and I wait for the commuters to pour out before I step onto the platform.

Connelly station throngs with rushing feet. I wait for the train to move away and then walk towards the gates. The ache in my leg is growing sharper. The clock over the exit reads 8:55 am.

*

The morning I left the hospital, the surgeon came to see me. His name was Patel. He stood over me for some time, manipulating my leg and then prodding and poking my hip.

'Any pain?'

I shook my head. 'No,' I lied.

'I think there is,' he frowned. There are no quick fixes, everything takes time.'

'I appreciate that.' After fourteen weeks I was eager to leave, but he hadn't finished.

'Nothing is so bad we can't fix it,' he said, his voice bright and authoritative.

I lifted my eyebrows, but he shook his head; we both knew he wasn't talking about my hip, arms, jaw or cheekbone, all of which he, and others, had repaired.

'We have people here,' he continued. 'Counsellors, good people.'

'I'll keep it in mind,' I said.

'Anyway, your leg and hip need to work now. To grow strong again, you need exercise — walk, walk, walk, everyday walk, first a little, then a little more.'

'Thank you, doctor.'

He shook my hand and turned away, and then as if in afterthought, turned back.

'Mr O'Neill, I don't want to see you on my operating table again.'

*

On the days I don't work, I walk along the sea road, or take the train to the city and walk from galleries to museums to libraries. On the nights I work, I get off the train one stop before the trading estate and walk along the footpath to the bridge. At first, I managed only short distances, now I can walk further. My leg is growing stronger and my body is healing.

But this morning my leg aches again. I slept poorly and woke early. I'm weary. But I have time so I will obey Patel's instruction and walk.

I limp past the taxi stand and along the pavement. Once across O'Connell street, I turn left past the GPO. The city hums, traffic passes, a bus brakes and hisses like an angry cat, horns blare. Shouts of anger and greeting merge into the air above the city. The wind carries the smell of exhaust, fast food, and burnt grain from the brewery.

I find the building. On the wall, a line of small plaques reflect the passing traffic. A chartered surveyor, a law firm, and the smallest of the plaques showing only her name, Dr Cathryn Ryan in bold black against the faux brass.

I press the intercom. A tinny voice answers,

'Cathryn Ryan's Office.'

'Dan O'Neill,' I say. 'I have an appointment.'

The door clicks and I push it inward and see the steps in front of me. I wince, then start the climb, using the crutch to steady myself.

Her office is on the second floor; by the time I reach the landing, I'm sweating. I can walk on flat pavement, but stairs are still difficult, forcing my right hip to work in a way it is not yet ready for.

A glass panel separates the reception from the landing. I step through an opening and am greeted by a round-faced young lady sitting behind a workstation. A tag on her ample breast announces her as Tiffany.

'You must be Daniel?' Her voice is bright and cheerful, her accent, pure mid-west American.

'Yes, I'm early.'

She clips a sheet to a board and turns it towards me.

'We need a few details, so take a seat.'

'I'd rather stand.'

I scribble my name, address, telephone number, then stall at 'Reason for your visit'. I leave it blank, sign and date the form and hand it back.

Tiffany takes it and looks up at me, smiling.

'She won't bite, you know.'

'Sorry?'

'Cathryn, she's nice, you look worried — you shouldn't be.'

'Thank you,' I smile.

The waiting area has a glass table and a white leather sofa. I take a seat and wait. The clock behind Tiffany reads 9:55 am.

Cathryn Ryan

I'd imagined her as middle-aged, frumpy, with wire-rimmed glasses on a stubby nose and, despite her name, a German accent. I would lie on a couch and she would perch, birdlike, beside me and ask questions. There would be flash cards with inky shapes — she would ask me to interpret them.

*

When the door behind Tiffany opens and Cathryn Ryan emerges, I am unprepared. She walks towards me, hand extended and smiling. Her hair is a dark rich red, tied back from her face. She wears a grey suit jacket and matching knee-length skirt.

In one detail I had been correct — her glasses, though they are black, horn-rimmed. She takes them off and extends her hand. Her eyes are grey–green with flecks of gold and rust.

'Dan. Thank you so much for coming in.' Her accent is English, Midlands, or West Country — I am not sure. I take her hand, it's cool and strong, her fingers tapered. I feel hardness, calluses, and imagine she gardens, or does something with wood, antique restoration, or perhaps she's a potter.

'Come on, let's get started.' She turns and I follow her into her office. Tiffany winks as I hobble by her desk.

*

Her room resembles a study rather than a doctor's

office. She's lined one wall with framed certificates, and below are pictures of Cathryn Ryan in boats: she is a rower — single sculls. One photo is black and white, an original of a media image, it shows her sitting in a boat on the water, an oar across her knee, grinning wildly and holding up a medal. Another shows her with a teenage girl — her daughter, I guess, as the resemblance is striking. They are both smiling into the camera; the doctor's arm is around the girl's waist and her hair is loose, falling over one shoulder. It is a studio shot, but a natural one.

A second wall is shelved, and books with gold leaf titles contrast with blue and red ring binders. Along the back wall is a coffee table with an L-shaped sofa, the same white leather as that in reception. All of this I take in as I stand in the office, balanced on my crutch.

'Come,' the doctor smiles, taking a seat at a wide desk. A phone, a computer and a neat stack of files sit to her left, but the surface is otherwise uncluttered. Behind her, a large leaded window frames the city. I see the crenellated top of the post office and beyond it the bridge, and wonder what the hell I am doing here.

I take my seat and she pulls a blue folder from the stack; I recognise my hospital file. It contains all my information — the damage, the cause, the repairs.

She looks at me curiously.

'You look like Maria.'

I grunt, surprised to hear my sister's name.

'So, you know her?'

'Yes, she was my patient for almost two years,

later we became friends.'

I feel my mouth twist into something between a smirk and a smile.

'Forgive me, Doctor … ' I begin.

'Cathryn, please call me Cathryn.'

I shrug.

'Ok, Cathryn. I'm still dubious about this, the letter, Maria?'

'Of course, it would be odd if you weren't.'

She hesitates for a moment. 'I'll be straight with you, Dan, this whole thing is unorthodox.' She frowns, joining her hands below her chin.

'Normally I wouldn't agree to become involved in something like … '

'Involved in what?' I lean forward. 'If Maria has something to tell me, why doesn't she just meet with me?'

Cathryn Ryan shrugs. 'She does want to meet you, but not yet.'

'Why?'

'She has her reasons, fear perhaps.'

'Fear of what? Of me?'

'Or for you.' Cathryn opens the file and flicks through it. She replaces her glasses and looks across the desk.

'It's your decision, Dan.' She looks up. 'No one can force you to go through with anything, but Maria has been clear about her conditions. If you are happy to accept them, I will help you.'

'Accept what?' I ask, exasperated. 'Psychoanalysis, head shrinking, what?'

She frowns, and a tracery etches the smooth plain

of her brow.

'If that's what you want to call it.'

'What if I say no?'

'Then I'll tell Maria I couldn't help.'

'And that will be that?' My voice is rising again.

'Perhaps, or maybe Maria will contact you anyway, or you her, I understand you have her mobile number.'

I say nothing for a while, considering..

'So, if I agree, how does this work? You ask me questions, I answer, and then what?'

'Yes. There will be questions, perhaps other therapies, but first I would need to know a lot more about you.' She pauses. 'You're not my patient, Dan, but that doesn't preclude me from exercising a duty of care. What we may do, and I say "may" advisedly, is complex. Delving into suppressed memories is not something I do lightly. There are risks associated with it, emotional and mental risks.'

She looks at me, her expression frank. She taps my file.

'You've been through a lot already.'

I nod but say nothing.

She opens the file.

'You have issues with addiction?'

'Yes. I was … am an addict.'

'And you've made one attempt on your own life?'

'Yes.' I look down at my hands. She's wrong, I didn't make an attempt on my life, or if I did, it was not an act of conscious will.

It had been a month after George died, and I'd returned to Dublin. I was on a ledge, looking down

21

over a city strewn with Christmas lights. I was drunk. Some image had flickered before me, and I'd stepped towards it, trying to grasp it, to understand it. Three days later I'd woken up in hospital with pain, noise and bright lights.

'So, you see, there are risks.' Cathryn Ryan smiled. 'I would be a poor doctor if I were to place you in danger.'

'You think I'm a suicide risk?' I shake my head. 'I'm not.'

She considers this, her eyes never leaving me.

'Are you sober now?'

'Yes.'

'For how long?'

'Since the twenty-second of December.'

'The night you jumped from the ledge?'

'The night I … ' I want to say fell, but I stop myself, and nod.

She closes the file, takes a card from a drawer and writes on it.

'Ok, here's what I propose. I would like to see you every morning for a week, starting next Monday. We will talk, and then when I know more about you, we can decide how to proceed.' She looks up. 'Are you willing to commit to that?'

'Do I have a choice?'

'There's always a choice, Dan.' She smiles, pushing her glasses up on her nose. 'What time is best for you?'

I shrug. 'Early?'

'Is 8:00 am ok?'

'That's fine.'

She hands me the card; it contains her name, office number and a cell number.

'I'll see you on Monday, then.' She leans across to shake my hand and I detect a scent of flowers, subtle but wonderful.

Elsewhere

I read off the number and key it in, then erase it for the fifth time. My throat is dry, my tongue feels like a slough of ash. .

The letter is open on the coffee table, turned over, the number underlined twice. I dial again, scowl and put the phone down and go to the fridge. I take a bottle of soda water, and drain it.

It's Thursday evening, six days after my visit to Cathryn and for several hours I've rehearsed my words, imagining what I will say and yet I haven't made the call.

What am I afraid of? Deep down I know that, as long as I don't call, there is hope — that all this is real, that Maria is alive. But if the voice that answers is not hers, what then?

I swear under my breath and clench my fists, angry at my own procrastination.

I grab the phone and punch in the numbers, my body tense. My hand is gripping the phone too tight, yet I cannot relax it. I hear the clicks, electronic signals moving through the ether, and she answers it on the second ring.

'Hello.' I wait, unsure, and the voice comes again.

'Hello?' I close my eyes. The voice is different, but there is a cadence to it, a rising inflection at the end that I recognise.

'Hello,' I say. My body is rigid and I'm shaking,

my breath catching in the hollow of my throat.

'Oh, my goodness, is that you, Danny?'

I nod, and then realise she can't see me.

'Maria?'

'Yes, Danny, it's me.' I hear her stifle a sob. 'It's so good to hear your voice.'

I open my eyes and feel the floor tilt beneath my feet; I close them again, grit my teeth, waiting for the dizziness to pass. I still don't know.

'Are you ok?' She asks, her voice quick, breathless. 'Did you go to see Cathryn?'

'Yes.' I speak at last. 'I did.'

'She's great, Danny. You can trust her, I promise.'

'I'm not sure,' I answer.

She says nothing, but I can hear her breathing, then the hiccup of another suppressed sob.

'Is it you?' I ask, my voice sounds hoarse.

'Yes, Danny. Yes, I swear it is. I know it's hard for you, and it's hard for me too. I want to tell you everything, but I'm terrified.'

'Why? What are you terrified of?' My voice is agitated. 'I need to see you, Maria, I need to know this is real.'

'I can't,' she whispers.

'Fuck that!' I'm angry now.

'After thirty years … After thinking all this time you were dead, don't you think I deserve that much?'

'I'm sorry. I can't.'

'Ok,' I say. 'I don't get this, any of it, but I'll play along. I've no choice.'

'There's always a choice, Danny.' Her words echo Cathryn's'

'I thought you'd come to Da's funeral,' she said finally. 'I waited, even after everyone else left. I stood in the church door, hiding, hoping I would catch sight of you. It was raining, and all I could think of was you.'

'By the time I found out, it was too late,' I answer. 'I was somewhere else.'

'Elsewhere.' She breathes the word. 'Wasn't that what we called it, Danny? Our escape. Elsewhere.'

I feel the tears stream down my face then, fat warm tears. Elsewhere. Would anyone else know?

'It's really you,' I say.

'Yes, Danny. It's really me.' She's crying and laughing.

*

Elsewhere. A name that came from what — a book, a movie? Maria would know; it was she who first called it 'Elsewhere', that place we escaped to.

Elsewhere, like the Catholic definition of heaven, is not just a place, but a state, a way of breathing, of moving. On those days when Ma screamed and broke things, when her breath stank of whiskey, when her hands became claws and her fists iron, Maria took me to Elsewhere.

She taught me to move like an automation, my passing disturbing only air. We became ethereal, ghosts that Ma's bloodshot eye would not detect.

When the familiar walls of our home turned dangerous, we merged into the background. We faded away. We drew the shallowest breaths and exhaled slowly and carefully because so long as we were Elsewhere, we were safe.

*

I sit at the breakfast bar, hunched over a coffee, considering her letter. For an hour, I've examined it, held it up to the light of reason, searching for fragments of truth, or flaws.

We'd spoken for only ten minutes, and I'd believed it was her. But once she hung up, the doubt returned.

The coffee steams, and I inhale the rising scent. It will keep me awake through a night's work. It's Thursday, and tomorrow morning I will visit Cathryn Ryan. It is the end of our first week. Will I get answers? I close my eyes at the futility of the question.

*

My job is menial. I take a list from a file and walk along aisles of high shelves, pulling cartons onto a battery-powered trolley. The trolley supports me, so I don't use the crutch.

When I've picked and assembled all the items on the list — biscuits, tea, washing powder — I drag the trolley to a packing station and transfer the order onto a wooden pallet on a turntable. Once assembled the turntable spins and plastic webbing wraps the pallet until it's coated in luminous blue. I hold the list in front of a scanner, a red light flashes and the machine produces a label which I attach to the shrink-wrapped pallet. I put the list in the finished tray and take a new list from the pending tray.

This is the total of my responsibility. The job is mundane, monotonous. They compile the lists in order with the layout of the shelving. Position numbers are printed on each line, so goods are easy to locate. It requires no thinking. Sometimes, I hit an out-of-stock item and use a headset to inform the warehouse. They tell me, via the headset, to continue picking the order and return later for the missing items or, if the warehouse is also out of stock, I place an X in a box and they will amend the order. It is important that the X runs from the corners of the box, and that it doesn't cross the line so the scanner can read it.

The job allows me time to think.

I finish work at 6 am, and each morning this week I've used the staff facilities to shower, change before catching the train back into the city. I've arrived at 8.00 am in Cathryn Ryan's office and sat for an hour answering questions. Cathryn insists my answers include details — I must recount events as though I am reliving them, describing what I see and feel. My emotional balance concerns her. She has spent the week breaking my life down into segments.

Her questions are about me; there's been little mention of Maria. I'm being accessed; Cathryn fears that if I begin the process without proper preparation, it may tip me over some invisible edge. I've stopped reassuring her. To her, I'm an addict and a suicide risk.

*

The hooter sounds. It's 3.00 am. I abandon my trolley and move towards the canteen where I join the queue of workers; we are all cogs in the machine, drones. There are fifty or more of us, at least three-quarters women, and most are Polish, Latvian or Croatian, part of the new wave of immigrants who come to Ireland in search of better lives. Most of them speak English, many fluently, but when they assemble in the canteen, they speak their native tongues.

I pour hot water from a boiler over instant coffee; I add milk and move to a bar that runs the length of one wall. There I sit and unwrap an egg and onion sandwich, ignoring the twitching noses. I have no particular fondness for egg or onion myself, except that eggs are easy to prepare and store; they hold together well and don't go off quickly. My decisions are based on what is easy and what is difficult; I shop for myself, and cook when necessary. I've learned to buy things that require little or no preparation. My freezer is small, but it accommodates half loaves of bread — a whole loaf will turn mouldy before I use it. It contains frozen fruit which I take out each night, filling a bowl with yoghurt for breakfast or lunch. I buy readymade salads in plastic bowls with plastic forks; the packaging is recyclable, so it comes with no baggage, practical or emotional.

This is what I've become, a creature of habit, an acolyte of a strict routine, filling my days and my nights with things to attend to. My body is free from damaging substances; I've been clean for almost eight months, the longest period for many years.

I toss my sandwich foil in the waste bin, then take my coffee back to the shelves where I sit on a broken pallet.

It's quiet away from the chatter of the canteen, the one the foreman calls Little Warsaw. I have not made friends in the job. I've been polite, answer when spoken to, but cultivated a sense of aloofness that my work colleagues respect.

Cathryn has broken my life into neat sections. The period after Ma and Maria's disappearance, up to and including the time I was with Da. Then the time I spent in Manchester, then Abbey Taylor. Thinking of Abbey makes me wince. After Abbey there are the years working with George before he died. And after that, Dublin, the damage, which she has listed as self-inflicted, and finally hospital and recovery.

Is this recovery? If so, what's beyond it? A return to my life?

The hooter sounds. I leave the empty coffee cup on the pallet and return to the aisles.

Roots of addiction

The blood that flows through my veins, that carries oxygen to my extremities and oils the pistons and valves of my limbs, carries with it a toxin of sorts.

My family history, from Caroline O'Neill (nee Caulk) backward, can be seen as a testament to the pervasive influence of deoxyribonuclease acid, the genetic code that passes from parent to child, imparting traits like blond hair, blue eyes, a talent for music, a gift for self-destruction.

I learned the Caulk history not on my mother's knee, but cowering at a distance, listening to drunken diatribes that started in bleary-eyed sweetness, eddied towards vitriol, and climaxed in rage. Passing to me through the veil of Elsewhere. My mother's words fragmented by time, gather and coalesce.

*

My great-grandfather was John Caulk, orphaned at eight years old, and at ten apprenticed to a quarryman in Co. Kilkenny. The year was 1849. John was big for his age, and before he was twelve he was wielding an eight-pound hammer.

Despite a lack of formal education, John Caulk was ambitious, and did not see himself as a quarryman. He was single-minded, with a head for figures and a flair for spotting opportunities.

When he was sixteen, he left the quarry and was hired by a monument works. He started as a labourer, but by the time he was thirty had learned how to cut and polish, shape and carve stone.

In 1870 John left Kilkenny and walked to Dublin, a distance of some eighty miles. He'd never earned a great deal of money, but he was frugal and had the better part of fourteen years' wages in his pocket. The journey took three days.

John arrived in the city late on Monday night. By Wednesday he'd found premisese in the new township of Glasnevin. He rented a cottage with land behind it and went about manufacturing blanks and samples.

Despite his frugality, he'd invested what he had in purchasing stone. He was on the verge of penury when he got his first important clients — a grieving couple who had lost a child to measles. A blow for them proved an opportunity for John.

The couple commissioned a substantial monument to be erected in the new cemetery close by and John took full advantage of the opportunity. The quality of his work was exceptional and soon he was in demand.

Over the following decade, John moved his works closer to the Port though he maintained the residence in Glasnevin, later buying the cottage and the land surrounding it. He grew rich, shaping and erecting headstones for the bereaved wealthy of Dublin, and when he died in 1919, they buried him in the same cemetery where much of his best work stood. His own headstone was a simple affair. The inscription read John Caulk 1838–1919.

Many attended his funeral, including friends, business acquaintances, and his wife Ester's family.

Four of John Caulk's surviving sons also attended, but the fifth son, William, who had been born the year his father turned fifty-one, was not among them. Though William had dressed for the occasion, Ester judged him too drunk to attend.

*

John Caulk had spoiled William. He had doted on the boy, denied him nothing, and wanted no other to take over his business, but the twenty-nine-year-old William was a drunk.

Despite his brothers' protestations and Ester's unflinching support, William drank and gambled the family business away within a year.

When Ester lay close to death, William was in Paris with his mistress. William's wife, Concepta, known to all as Connie, was sitting by Ester's death bed when her mother-in-law sat up and grasped her hand.

'Don't blame him. He's sick,' she said, and Connie knew Ester spoke of William.

Ester passed a purse into Connie's hand. 'You must never tell him I gave it to you,' she whispered, 'or even that you have it.'

It was a day before Connie realised that Ester had given her what amounted to almost £3000. It was 1920.

*

William died of syphilis in London in 1922, penniless. It would be a year before Connie learned of her husband's passing. She didn't mourn him; in fact, she'd all but forgotten him. She dedicated herself to the care of her twelve-year-old son Michael, and the rebuilding of the fortune her husband had squandered.

Connie Caulk knew nothing about stone, so she turned her attention elsewhere. She made an ally of a young man who had caught her eye, the son of prosperous undertakers.

Ester convinced the young swain to leave his father's employmente and work with her. It's possible he believed she promised more than a business partnership but Connie, once bitten, was not inclined to try her hand at marriage a second time.

Between 1922 and 1927 Connie learned enough about the business of funeral directing to enter the trade alone.

In January 1928 she opened a small premise in Inchicore under the name of William Caulk and Son. When the business opened, Michael was eighteen and already a notorious drunk.

*

Despite her growing business, illness, and advancing age, Connie did everything she could to prevent Michael from following the same path as his father. Over the next several years she would have him committed to asylums and limit the money he had access to, but Michael proved resourceful. When he took to crime, Connie paid his debts, but only on condition that he would reform.

Amidst the chaos that was his life, Michael impregnated Hettie, the daughter of a hotelier, and swearing he loved her, married her. The marriage kept him focused for a period and when his daughter, Caroline, who would become my mother, was born, Connie saw hopeful changes in him. However, before Caroline was a year old, Hettie, a weak and wan girl who had never recovered from childbirth, succumbed to consumption. Michael, heartbroken, found comfort in whiskey.

*

While Michael attempted to drink himself into an early grave, he left Caroline in the care of an ageing Connie.

Caroline grew up among the dead. They didn't frighten her, and often at night she sat quietly in the shop, reading a novel or writing her diary, the bodies of the deceased her only company. She seldom thought of her father, and when she did, she recalled him as a drunk.

Perversely, Michael Caulk, my grandfather, found his salvation in 1939, when World War II broke out. Michael, drunk but full of patriotic zeal and armed with false papers that showed his age at ten years less, left Caroline in the care of his mother and joined the army. All that's known of him after that is through his letters — from England, then France and later Poland. He remained sober for the duration of his service and was promoted to Sergeant.

Michael wrote to Connie often, but never mentioned the horrors in Poland, nor did he speak of the awfulness of war; instead he outlined plans for his return, how he would settle down and help Connie, how he would ensure Caroline got a good education.

His last letters came from Cracow in August 1942. The same day he handed it over to the postmaster, he stood on a landmine. The letter from the British army outlined the details of his service and his bravery, expressing sympathy for Connie and Caroline and suggesting how they might claim his effects. There were no remains to bury.

*

On the day her father died, Caroline was six years old.

Two years after Michael's death, Connie Caulk experienced severe chest pains. A combination of stress and obesity caused the heart attack. It was massive, and it is likely that Connie felt little. Caroline was alone, and had few immediate relatives. A second cousin took custody of her, against his will.

Unlike her father who found his salvation in war-torn Poland, Caroline would experience no event that would move or change her, neither in her young life or marriage, nor in the birth of her children.

Stepping back

The train pulls into Connolly station and, as always, I wait for others to disembark before I step out onto the platform. My leg aches this morning. I walk to the exit, hesitate, then shuffle past the taxis. It would be too easy to engage one, but easy is a slope, easy is a kind of surrender.

*

'You haven't been completely straight with me, Dan,' says Cathryn. 'However, we need to move on.'

'What? You think I lied?'

'No, that's not what I said. I think you've … omitted things.'

*

So far, I've spent a week outlining the events of my life: before Dublin, then the aftermath. Cathryn is a good listener; she seldom interrupts other than to clarify a point. She takes notes and adds them to a growing file.

'So, what's next?' I ask.

Over the week we have become familiar; our relationship is not that of therapist and client. There are subtle differences — a kind of dissonance that punctuates our conversations, questions asked that might otherwise not be. Cathryn challenges me to examine myself. She does not treat me as though I'm fragile, nor does she allow me to dictate the flow of our hourly sessions. She is quick to correct me, and insists I delve deeper, that I talk about how the events I recall affected me and how, over the years I've reacted to disappointment, fear, love and heartbreak.

I wait for her to answer my question.

'We take the next step.' She hesitates and I wonder why.

'We go backward,' she replies, her eyes locked on mine.

'Ok.' I shrug. 'But how?'

'Go back to the house.'

*

I feel the blood draining from my face.

'Our old house?' My voice is tremulous. 'Is it still there?'

'Yes, but not for much longer, as it's to be demolished next week.'

She waits until I return her stare.

'Are you willing to go?'

'Will it help?' I ask.

'I believe so. Maria does, too.'

'Ok, yes, I'll go.'

'When?'

'On Sunday.'

Even as I answer, the dread sits like a rock in the pit of my stomach. I'm frightened that the past might consume me, that it will reach out and damage me further.

Cathryn smiles and slides an envelope across the table.

'Maria asked me to give this to you.'

It's large, A4, with 'Danny' written across it, underlined twice. I recognise the hand: it's that in which the letter that still sits folded in my pocket is written.

I pick it up, and I pull out the single sheet: a glossy photograph. I stare at it, lost in the image. It's professionally done, the background plain black, matching her clothing, so drawing my eye to the brightness of her face and the exposed V of her neck.

She is looking at the camera. A vivid scar runs across her left cheek. She is older; still beautiful but not with the bright, newly minted innocence of a teenager; she is weather-worn, tanned and touched by life. There are care marks about her forehead and the corners of her mouth. But her eyes are the same and when I look into them, she seems to be staring straight back at me. Maria. My sister — different, older, but it's her, and she is alive.

*

'Will you go alone?' Cathryn asks as I slide the photo back into the envelope.

'Yes, I think so.' I don't add that there is no-one to accompany me, no friends or associates, or even acquaintances.

'Ok, I'll be home all day. Michael is not coming home this weekend and Jen is staying at a friend's house on Saturday night.'

She's referring to her husband and her daughter. In the past five days, I've been a silent witness to several telephone calls from her daughter, questions about books, or school socks or the whereabouts of various items. I've sat through one telephone conversation with her husband that sounded fractious. Afterwards, Cathryn apologised and explained that she kept her mobile on because Michael was working in the UK, and Jennifer was often alone.

I am not her patient; she is doing me a service although it is at my sister's request. Cathryn said that Maria was her friend; I'm an addendum to that friendship. I'm certain she views me as odd, eccentric even; she smiles at my self-deprecation, and nods at my efforts to stay sober. I cannot define our relationship, but we're not friends and she is not my doctor.

'Call me if you need to talk, or anything else.'

'I will,' I assure her. It's almost 9 am. Cathryn walks me to the door. She shakes my hand; it feels warm and reassuring.

'Good luck.' She leans in close; her perfume is heady, earthy. 'Come in on Monday, as early as you like.'

'I'm free from 5.30,' I joke. I don't work Mondays, but I'm used to being awake at night and sleeping days.

She shrugs.

'Ok,' she says as though it's not out of the ordinary. 'I'll bring coffee.'

*

On Fridays I don't go to bed after work. Instead, I stay up, fighting sleep. I fall into bed when the day leaches from the sky, and sleep through the hours of darkness. This allows me to make the most of Saturdays.

After leaving Cathryn's, I wander into town. It's cheaper for me to shop in the city than in the satellite where I live, and shopping keeps me awake.

I waste several hours walking the aisles of discount stores. I need little, but I pick up items and put them back again because it occupies my mind. Images of the house encroach but I push them aside. I will face it on Sunday, but I want no truck with it until then.

After exhausting the possibilities of the discount stores and eating a slow lunch in the city, I catch a train back to the studio a little after four o'clock. I stow the bread and the eggs, placing the onions and tomatoes in the vegetable tray of the fridge. I take the frozen fruit out and place the fresh purchased bags to the back.

The studio is not dirty, but it is untidy. I strip the bed and remake it; it's too late to go to the laundromat and too early to stay in so I walk back to the station and take the first train back into the city. By the time I return, I'm tired and though my mind is full of what's to come, I fall asleep.

*

On Saturday I clean the studio. I wash down the kitchen units, clean the fridge, vacuum the wooden floor and mop it. I take the bed linen to the laundromat, spending an hour walking there and back and another hour washing and drying, my eyes fixed on the hypnotic spinning of the machine.

In the afternoon I make sure the car starts; I haven't used it in weeks, but it turns over at the first try. It's old, I bought it when I rented the studio because I wasn't sure where I'd be working, but it was cheap and in good condition, so I've kept it. I spend an hour polishing the dash and vacuuming the seats and then I turn towards the sea.

A lane runs at the side of the park, crossing a main road and ending at stone steps leading down to the coast. At the end of the steps is a path of limestone blocks. I walk towards the island — it shimmers in the distance, cloud shadows race across the links and the roughs, and a warm wind whips off the sea. I zip up my coat and dig my hands into my pockets. I've not brought the crutch as I'd not intended to walk any distance, but within an hour I'm standing on the edge of a headland. North, along the coast, Howth rises like a crouching beast, and to the south is the distinctive outline of the Sugarloaf, its summit bright beneath rays of fractured sun.

My leg is stiff, I've done too much. I pat the pocket of my jacket and hear the rattle of pills. I've not used them for over a week but carrying them reassures me. The walk back takes longer.

At the studio, I pour tinned soup into a pot and, while it heats, butter three slices of bread. I'm tired; the pain in my leg has worn me down. I set the bread and soup down on the breakfast bar, then I sit to eat, and contemplate the final two clues in the cryptic crossword which I'd abandoned the previous weekend, and solve them quickly. I curse because I haven't bought a paper today. I own a radio but no TV. The studio is quiet, and the silence is, for once, oppressive.

Da

Da was holding my hand, something he hadn't done since I was small. It was hard and callused, but warm and reassuring. I did not pull mine away.

We were standing in the front room; the hearth was cold grey ash, and the floor was shining.

Da only spoke once, his voice low and unsteady.

'Come on, Danny.'

He carried a small suitcase with a tartan cover; I had nothing. I'd not gone to the loft to get clothes. When I turned towards the kitchen, Da's hand tightened on mine.

We left the house.

The thud of the front door closing sounded like a nail hammered home, and Da didn't turn to lock it. He took my hand, squeezed it, then walked in that quick way of his, past the feather-house, the machine shed and into the yard.

*

We went to live with my Uncle Paul.

My father had always been a small man, but broad and muscular; he took pride in his appearance, was always neat and dapper. In the first months, maybe in the first year, I didn't see the change in him; I was too young and my own loss too raw. He was different, yes; he worked on the Mary J with Paul, and when ashore he paid more attention to me. We spoke every day and I became accustomed to it, but he never spoke about the thing I most wanted to discuss and so, I stopped asking.

*

I changed too; I grew fast with my fists and developed a strong chin and a smart mouth. Da did all he could to keep me out of trouble, but he couldn't protect me from myself.

I left school the following year. Da tried to talk me out of it, but soon gave up. At fifteen, I took my place on the Mary J. There wasn't work for three and so, after a month teaching me, Da stayed ashore.

At night, I dreamed, tossed, shouted and swore, waking to the sound of my aunt rocking the crying baby, hushing her back to sleep. Mary Josephine O'Neill, my Aunt Josie, feared me; I had brought brooding darkness to her house. She watched me as though I were something feral and unpredictable, cradling the baby, protecting her.

Paul tried, treating me as kindly as any uncle might. I'm sure he loved me, but he could not protect me.

Da took to sitting on the harbour, waiting for the Mary J to land. I'd see his silhouette as we rounded the point, crouched forward, as though searching the sea below the pier. As we drew closer, he'd stay sitting, his head turning towards the red bow rail of the boat, searching for me. I should have waved back every day, and wished later that I had. But I was ashamed of what he had become. He sat on the rusted bollard, a dirty blue cap on his head, the peak pulled low, his face grey with stubble. And when he stood, he looked like an old man, his movements cautious, feeble. He wore the same clothes most days — a green jumper, threadbare at the elbows, brown corduroy pants that sagged at the arse and the knee, and dirty torn tennis shoes, laces loose or open.

He'd never been heavy, but during those final two years he became gaunt, his face shrunken, and eyes lined and recessed. He was collapsing in on himself and, lost in my own pain, I turned away from his.

*

Josie wanted me gone. She minded Da, cared for him, but my dark moods frightened her. I didn't blame her . There was too much of Ma in me, too much blood that fizzed and popped, too much ire.

I never raised a hand in anger in her house, but there had been too many years of our not knowing each other. I was a stranger, a shadow cast over their lives.

It was Paul who told me to go, but I knew it was Josie who wanted it. He told me there was nothing in the village for me, that I'd be better off away from it, and as he spoke I heard all the things he didn't say, saw them in the set of his jaw and in his eyes, squinting towards the horizon line.

*

Da was sitting on the bed in a room that reflected nothing of him. There were no clothes on chairs, no photographs or mementos; he laid no claim to the space he occupied. He was so small, as vulnerable as a child.

His hands reached out, like the grasping talons of a small bird, soft, sharp, with so little flesh. His fingers grasped mine, the lightest tug as he pulled me closer, the rasp of his stubble against my cheek, the wetness of tears. It was that which shocked me most; I'd never seen him cry. And now, I convince myself that it was because of tears that I didn't leave him as I should have.

He pushed me away, not with force but firmly. His hand lingered on my chest, his shrunken eyes looking into mine.

'Go,' he rasped. 'Go, Danny, forget it all, the place, the house, me, your Ma, forget everything.'

When I looked back from the door, he was sitting on the bed again, shoulders slumped. It was the last time I saw him. It would be years later before I learned what he absorbed, so I could be free of it.

A day later I went to Manchester. I was eighteen years old.

*

Eventually I slept, and the memories did not follow me into my slumber, nor did the fear. When I woke, I left the studio, fooling myself that I was ready for the day ahead.

Filth

I crawl back, like an injured animal seeking its lair. And when I close the door behind me, there is no relief. It clings to me. The house, the mire. The stench on my clothes, in my hair, and the dirt and dust in my body and lungs make me retch.

I strip naked, throwing my clothes into the basket, then taking them out again, I get a sack from under the sink and bundle them into that, replacing them in the basket. Tomorrow I will take them to the laundromat and wash the ichor of the house from them.

My hands are filthy, palms black and sticky from the shit and piss of vermin, and something worse — the residue of damaged lives, greasy beneath my nails. My skin is itchy from the dust and grime, but I'm afraid to scratch.

The water cascades over me and I turn the handle until I burn and still it's not enough. I shampoo my hair once, and then again, lather running down my body. I use a nail brush, scrubbing my fingers until the quicks bleed but still, when I lift my hands to my nose, it's there, beneath the soap and scent of sandalwood … the stench of the house. I douse my body with shower gel and scrub every inch of my skin, rubbing my scars raw. The water cools but I still feel it, like the rasp of a blade. I scrub more. The water goes cold and my body grows pink from scrubbing, but I can still smell it, taste it.

I get out of the shower and towel myself dry, rubbing it over my hair, working it between my fingers and my toes. I apply deodorant everywhere, desperate to rid myself of the stink of decay, of the things that brushed against my face like fingers reaching out for me. I brush my teeth so hard they bleed.

I pull pyjamas from my small closet. It's cold now. Outside it's dark, and the wind has picked up and sings through the park railings. I'm tired and my leg is throbbing; I want to ring Maria but I have nothing to tell her. There was nothing in the house that I didn't already know. I look at the green LED on the radio: it's ten minutes to midnight. I only have a few hours before I need to be up. Tomorrow I will see Cathryn; perhaps she can tell me what it was I missed.

*

Cathryn sits back, hands steepled, index fingers tapping her chin.

'Tell me from the start.' Her voice is soft, and flows over me like balm.

She's staring at me. Her eyes are the lightest smokey grey, and when the sun glints I see shades of gold .

I grunt and lean forward, resting my elbows on my knees, not thinking. The pain shoots through my right thigh. I sit back up and reach for the pills in my pocket but her eyes still my hand.

She's waiting. Waiting for me to tell her a story.

But where to begin? Not at the start, to go there would be to expose to much of myself, but I can't go

48

to the end either, because the story is still unfolding. So I start at the place she sent me to.

*

'A phrase kept repeating. A quote. Or rather the tail end of a quote.'

She's watching me, waiting. And now I'm sorry I started here.

'What was the quote?'

'And if you gaze long enough into an abyss, the abyss will gaze back into you.'

'Nietzsche?' She smiles at me and leans forward to scribble something on her pad. 'Why that quote?'

'You're the psychiatrist.' I raise an eyebrow, and she nods for me to go on.

I continue and, as I do, she closes her eyes.

'I hummed the lyrics of a song, that just an hour ago I could not dislodge from my head, but it won't settle. I tried repeating a stanza of a poem. But Nietzsche, the bastard, was still whispering in my ear.'

It's Cathryn's turn to raise an eyebrow. She doesn't like me swearing when I come to see her; I shrug in apology.

'My leg was aching, I did too much on Saturday, so I focused on the pain.'

'Good.'

The damage to my leg is healing, but the past few days have seen it throb again. I recall leaving the hospital; it was April, the cherries along Eccles Street were shedding pink petals that blew in swirls along lines of sun and shadow. Now it's September and the promise of that spring day is replaced by lacklustre trees and muggy heat. A line of sweat forms between my shoulders and my eyes feel scratchy and sore.

'Did you drive out on your own?' She writes on her pad again, waiting for me to answer.

'Yes. I thought it would be ok, it only took an hour.'

'How did you feel, seeing it all again?'

'It was ok. It's changed, the road is a proper street now, they've removed old toe-paths, and hedges too. There are footpaths, you know — pavement, tarmac and kerbstones.'

I don't tell her how I deluded myself on the journey out. And how, despite Nietzsche and my leg flexing and throbbing, I'd hoodwinked myself into believing that I was going nowhere in particular, that my journey was one I chose to make. But who drives to the edge of the map by choice?

I recall my hands clasping the wheel just before I reached the crossroads, my fingernails biting into my palms, the pain reassuring me that I was still in control, that I could drive on, follow the road to the next town and the one after that and never look back.

She tuts. 'I don't need those details, Dan. I'd rather know how you felt, and what your first impressions were. And please relate it in the way I asked you to.'

Cathryn wants me to relive each detail as I speak, to put myself back in the scene and describe it as if it is happening now.

I close my eyes.

'As I entered the village, the sun came out from behind a cloud — like a holy thing, a revelation. The light and shadow paint a shimmering grey and black fresco on the wall of a white house that crouches on the right corner of the crossroad. Between the light and dark, men shimmered; they were not real, but shadows — only for a moment, but I recognised them, the ghosts of garrulous old men, fuckers, men who knew too much and admitted too little. Then I blinked and they dissolved. How's that for crazy?'

I open my eyes and she is still sitting back. She doesn't bother chiding me for swearing this time.

'There were changes,' I continued, without being asked. 'Like the roads, a new footpath, lots of new houses. They take up most of the road frontage.'

'So did you go to the house?'

'Not straightaway. I wasn't ready. I drove past and went to the harbour first.'

'The boat?'

I don't answer.

'Was it there?'

I still don't reply. I think of the sea heaving, the dark slate grey under a mackerel sky, its mass and solidity throwing back light that made me squint. A part of me was still convinced that I had a choice, that I might return to the city, have lunch on Grafton Street, and later walk through St Stephen's Green.

*

'Tell me about the old men.' She looks at the pad, reading her own notes. 'What did you mean when you said they knew too much but admitted to too little?'

I curse myself for not sticking to the facts. She wants details, feelings, words and deeds, scents and tastes. I have become accustomed to talking to her in

51

a certain way, and now I've trapped myself.

'Where did you grow up?' I asked.

'Lincoln. But, we're not here to talk about me, Dan.' She grins, looking suddenly younger.

'Is that a big town?'

'Yes.'

'Well then, you won't understand.'

She smiles at this. 'Tell me anyway.'

And so I try.

'Small villages have a way of not doing or seeing a thing, not talking about them either, while still seeing and doing and talking.'

'Like what? What sort of things?'

The sun is visible through the window behind her, colouring the sky pink and red; soon it will rise over the buildings and shine straight down on me. She'd come in at 5.00 am to see me, and scheduled three hours instead of our normal one.

'Like anything that shames them,' I answer.

I look away. She scowls, but she's clever, and knows if she waits that I'll feel compelled to fill the silence. She knows so much about me and yet beyond the fact that she is from a large town, English and married with a daughter, I know so little about her.

Her face remains impassive.

'They, all of them … covered things up. Things that are meant to be secret, but really aren't … but they might just as well be, because nobody acknowledges them.'

She is about to speak, and I know I am procrastinating, avoiding her question.

'Rape, incest, pedophilia. You name it, Cathryn.

52

Child abuse, alcoholism, drug addiction, all the things that happen behind closed doors, things that no one reports, because how can you report your brother or your cousin? It's all plastered over with platitudes.'

'Ok, I see. Go on, you drove through the village?'

'I drove past the old school.' I visualise the white pebble dash with a sooty stained patina, its grey slate roof greened with moss. Its windows, like blank eyes staring out at a yard of grass, and the indelible scuff marks of students carved about its edge. Children once played there, kicked balls and fought with fists and kicked with boots and sandals and pointy brogues, and dirty fingernails scratched and cut and drew blood. Inside, boys sat in one row, girls in another, all learning by rote:

4. Honour thy father and thy mother.
5. Thou shalt not kill.

I shudder.

'It was abandoned,' is all I say.

I don't tell her about the new school. The redbrick, multi-gabled building, flanked by two play areas, black tarmac to the left, and soft green and ocher surface that doesn't scratch knees or draw blood to the right. A lawn stretched from the brick walls of the school, to the fence that fronts to the road. Hypericum lined the path from the gate to the twin entry doors, their large cupped flowers of a deep glistening yellow, absorbing the early light and returning it brighter.

Nor do I tell her that at the farthest corner of the children's playground, where goalposts stood, the shadow of the old building crept across the asphalt, a dark malignant stain, the old stretching towards the new.

'And the harbour?' she asks.

'It's still the same. Only at the end of the road did I see any real difference. There used to be open fields, and fishermen's houses there but they're gone. There are new houses — two large ugly ones, all white and blue and glowing steel, ultramodern.'

I think of their walls, built at odd angles to track the sun, and windows, octagonal and hexagonal, trims painted Mediterranean blue.

'They were discordant,' I say, and grimace at my choice of words. 'Out of place, like they were trying to be better than those around them.'

'The houses, or the people who live in them?'

'Neither. It was a silly thing to say, they seemed … I don't know, pretentious.'

Cathryn lifts the pen again and scribbles a note. I've said something to cause her pause.

'There's a new carpark, and the harbour has a gate … no, not a gate, one of those barriers that you need a swipe card or keypad so it lifts.'

'But you can still walk to it?'

'Yes. But I didn't. I sat in the car and looked out at the beach.'

'Can you see the harbour from the beach?'

She is unrelenting. She will not ask directly, but she will lead me until I get to where I need to go.

I think about the beach, the tide ebbing and the sand stretching towards it like the wet hide of some dead creature, laid out to dry.

'Just the furthest extent,' I answer. 'It bends or rather curls, like the upper part of a question mark.' My right hand draws the shape in the air. 'It stretches out across the mouth of the bay, and the inner wall is where the boats tie up.'

I recall the line of trawlers rising and falling, tethered on the end of blue and orange painter ropes.

The sun rises over the buildings behind Cathryn, a low cloud blunting its light, but soon she will have to draw the shades.

'Tell me what you saw as you sat in your car.'

I told her about the beach, the sea, and harbour.

'There were men moving about a boat, all of them dressed in orange and yellow oilskins.'

'Did you speak to them?'

She pulls her notebook closer and gestures for me to answer.

'I didn't want to see them, not then. Maybe never.'

I couldn't explain this part to her, but as I sat watching them, a dark cloud moved across the sun and I caught my own reflection in the windscreen. My face was long and gaunt, my jaw jagged and my eyes deep wells of darkness, shadows that looked like bruises. I looked like Da; I wanted to turn away from them and in doing so, from myself.

I give her something in place of honesty.

'The Mary J was close to the top of the harbour. I only saw a part of her ... her stern.'

'Did you want to go nearer, to look at her up close?'

'No.' I shake my head.

'You weren't at all curious?'

'No. I wasn't.' I sound gruff.

She hesitates; she knows I'm lying, and she knows I know it.

She exhales.

'So what did you do next?'

'I drove to the house.'

The sun has cleared the clouds and is now dazzling. She stands and moves towards the window to adjust the shade. Her suit today is grey and white pinstripe, the jacket of a light material that crackles with static as she moves; it clings to her, the skirt hugging her hips. Her hair from behind is a froth of loose curls that glisten like embers in the light.

I've told her part of the story; I left out the school. I left out the phone call too, though for no good reason.

*

When I turn to leave the carpark, the phone vibrates in my pocket. I had to dig for it, stretching my hand into my jeans pocket. A jolt of pain runs up my leg. I'm breathless by the time I answer. It's Maria.

'Danny, are you there?'

'Yes.'

'Have you gone to the house yet?'

'No, not yet.'

'Will you?'

Would I? I still don't know, but that isn't what she wants to hear.

'Yes, I will, but I drove to the harbour first.'

'What's it like, the village? Has it changed much?'

'No, it's the same as it ever was,' I answer

impatiently, and in pain, but I know that she would have noticed the changes.

I hang up and take the pills from my pocket. I dry swallow two and sit back for a moment, my pulse as loud as the waves washing over the wet sand. The Mary J is visible in my rearview mirror, her nose buried in the mud of the shallows.

The house

'So, the house. Tell me about it, did you go inside?'

She's still standing, stretching, breasts tight against her white blouse. I notice her hands, tanned, long tapered fingers, nails cut short. I imagine her skimming on the water, straining against an oar, her hair streaming over her face.

'Yes, but it took a little while. I wasn't sure if I could get to it at all.'

*

I had sat for a long while at the entrance to the lane, still believing I could reverse out onto the street and drive away, that I had a choice. I turned the key, but turned it back without starting the engine. I hadn't unbuckled the seatbelt though it was cutting into my lap, and pain flared up from my right hip, a dull ache, making me nauseous.

*

Cathryn watches me, her eyes wide.

'There was a white notice nailed to a fence post at the entrance, hammered into the verge. Two concrete blocks propped it up.' I hesitate.

'It was at the edge of the property line. I wondered if the men who had erected it had known something, or if they had sensed what lay further in.'

'Do you believe that's possible?'

A laugh rises within me, but I suppress it.

'No, they put it there because the lane was

overgrown,' I lie.

When I'd seen the overgrowth, I'd imagine the teeth of a mechanical digger ripping it all away, revealing the grey stone beneath, clawing its way towards the house and the barn.

'The sign was a planning notice,' I tell her.

'The builder John McCarthy is to erect eight four-bedroom houses … you know.'

'How did you feel about that?'

'The sign wasn't the artist's best work. It was a typed notice, on white paper and laminated, but the nail driven through had rusted, and the paper was all orange-stained and wrinkled.'

Her mouth creases in a half smile.

'About the houses they intend to build, Dan.'

I imagine those homes, as I had done when I stood at the end of the lane, thinking of the families that would occupy them, never knowing the dark things that inhabit the soil beneath their new L-shaped kitchens or their split-level dining rooms, and unaware of the ghosts that live in the soil beneath their children's bedrooms, the things that might crawl up to the surface on moonless nights.

'I hope they are luckier than we were.'

I can tell by her eyes that she doesn't believe me, but she doesn't press me.

'So, what did you do?'

'Like I said, the lane to the house was a wilderness of briar and thorn, the heads of lank thistles poked out from the top. The only part of the house visible was the chimney, the terracotta capping, split and leaning down. It would have been easier to wait for the diggers to clear it.'

'But if you waited, it would have been too late.'

'Yes,' I shrug. 'It would have been too late.'

'So, you waded in?'

I roll up my left sleeve and show her the scratches and scrapes where thistles and thorns had left bloody lines. I didn't show her where briar ripped my shirt and my jeans, snagging me as though pulling me back. Or talk about the sweat running down my forehead and neck and the pulsing nausea that beat against my ribs and throat.

'I took an hour to get halfway,' I said. 'When I looked back, I couldn't see the road. I could see only fragments of the car through the whips that sprung up behind me. I doubt anyone on the road would have seen or heard me, but I could hear them — traffic and the voices of children out early playing on the street, dogs barking — the village waking.'

Cathryn nods, dropping her pen.

I tell her about the cat. It mewed first, then I saw it stalking away from me, black and white, with its tail held aloft, disdainful of my intrusion, perhaps. I'm sure it is a descendent of a large cat called Gráinneog — a black and white tiger that had spat when I came near it. It only allowed Da to stroke it, and then only for a moment before strutting away.

And I tell her about a blue ball in the tangle, scarred with teeth marks. The dog's name had been Jess — a mongrel Collie that sat by the door, running to greet us when we came home from school, but freezing whenever Ma spoke.

I don't tell her how my body ached or how red

60

and itchy my hands were from the briars and thistles; how a thorn ripped a ragged line in my shirt and blood seeped through; or how the raw purple lines, where the surgeons cut me, throbbed. I also don't tell her that I'd popped two more pills; how frightened I felt of addiction and how I was already well over my quota for the day.

'You got to the house?'

'Yes.'

*

I think of how the sounds of the village receded, and all I could hear was the rustling of feral things, resentful of my intrusion, and the cry of gulls flashing overhead, with their black beaded eyes , combing the disturbed earth and foliage, sweeping down to pluck out the things I'd unearthed.

*

'It took time,' I continue. 'I didn't realise how soft my body became in the hospital. I was sweating, my chest bursting — my leg was hurting like a bitch. By the time I saw the roof, my hip was a raw, burning ache.'

Cathryn says nothing but her eyes are on me, the corners of her mouth soft.

'The last part was the hardest. My arms were heavy, weary from the effort of using the light aluminium crutch to beat the briar down and balance my body. The scars of the surgery tightened and burned. It was only the sight of weathered, gap tooth sheets on a sagging roof that keeps me moving.'

I pause. 'It would have been easier to wait for the diggers,' I repeat. But I knew the journey had to begin and end before the diggers came.

'I beat down the last of the thorns. The trees behind the house loomed over it, threatening to overwhelm it. But the yard in front was bare, the ground there had become too compacted or too toxic for anything to grow.'

I moved to ease the ache in my leg and groan.

'Are you ok? Do you need a cushion or anything?'

I don't respond, telling her instead the last bit.

'The door was at the side of the house, so I couldn't see it. I stood there for a long time, waiting, and then I walked towards it. I saw The Lady in the Glass.'

'Ok.' She holds up her hands. 'Let's take a break.'

She stands and stretches, catching me eyeing her breasts, but says nothing.

'Coffee?'

I grunt and use the crutch to stand. 'Yes, please.'

'Let's move to the sofa, I need to lounge,' Cathryn smiles. She will not talk about the house while we take a break, but moves to safer territory, less important matters.

I find it hard to sit; the sofa's too low, and I'm forced to stretch my leg out in front of me.

Cathryn sits and kicks off her shoes, rubbing her left foot. Her feet are small and neat, the soles hard — runner's feet.

'Are you sure we're ready for this?' I smile, eyeing her feet.

'What? Do you have a foot fetish, Dan?'

I laugh, and her hand goes to her chin, half-hiding her smile and her eyes become crystalline. I realise that outside of this office she is a different person, one that I do not know at all.

Tiffany comes in with the coffee. A tray with a steaming pot, two cups and a milk jug.

She smiles at me. I'm surprised to see her in the office so early.

'How are you, Dan?'

'Oh, you know,' I answer, returning her smile. 'Still bat shit crazy.'

Her smile grows wider. 'I doubt it,' she shoots back. 'But hey, there are worse ways to be.'

I've grown fond of Tiffany; she's all bright-eyed innocence, with an openness that appeals.

'So, how's the job, Dan?' Cathryn asks.

I look at her. She's curled one foot beneath her and holds her coffee between cupped hands, and looks contented.

'We're off the clock,' she winks. 'It's just a friendly question.'

I talk about the warehouse where I assemble stuff I have no interest in. I explain how it's boring but pays the rent and feeds me, and how I enjoy working nights when the world is sleeping, and being invisible during the day. I don't tell her how, at first, I'd save up my pills so I could get through the nights. Or that I will soon quit the job.

'Have you made any friends?'

'Are we still off the clock?'

She blushes. 'Sorry, force of habit.'

I respond anyway. 'It's hard, the people I work with are not like me, they talk about kids, domestic stuff, they are mostly immigrants.'

'Does that bother you?'

'Are you asking if I'm a racist?'

'No. I meant that they are different, that you're not part of the clique.'

I nod, smiling. Her embarrassment feels like a victory in this game where I am so often exposed, and she is a mystery.

'No, I'm content in the job and the people I work with are fine — they're friendly, I get on well with them. But I don't need friendship just now, that comes with certain expectations — invitations to things, nights out, phone calls.' I shrug. 'I can't deal with all that now. So, the job is perfect, and the isolation suits me.'

'What about women, a girlfriend? Are you seeing anyone?'

I laugh at this, and it turns into a cough. 'Christ, no.'

Something moves behind her eyes, and she blinks.

'Is it hard?' she asks.

'What, the job, or no woman in my life?'

Cathryn places her empty cup on the floor.

'Well, you're not an old man, you have needs ... ' She pauses. 'As we all do.'

'A relationship would be a distraction.'

She stands.

'Let's get started again.' She looks down at me. 'Would you rather move back to the desk or stay on the sofa?'

I make to stand, but the pain flares and I drop back down.

'Here, I guess.'

She slips her shoes back on and goes to the desk,

returning with the seat I'd used earlier.

She sets it close and sits, her profile silhouetted, as the sun flares from the window.

*

'Let's talk about Abigail.'

'Why? What's Abbey to do with this?'

'Trust me, Dan. It's important.'

'Is it about rejection?' I ask. 'Are you curious about how I will react to it? Or is it more duty of care?'

She's staring at me with those grey eyes, wide and honest.

'Do you think Maria might reject me — might refuse to see me?'

'I think it is more likely you might reject her.'

'Why would I?' I lean forward. 'She's my sister. I love her, I want to see her.'

'She may not be all that you expect, Dan.'

'Explain that,' I demand. But she shakes her head.

'Let's cross that bridge when we come to it, ok?' There is steel in her tone, so I sit back, grunt and close my eyes, but the truth is it will be easier to talk about Abbey than about the house or Maria.

'Ok, let's start with how you met her. It was in Manchester, yes?'

Manchester

'It was afterwards,' I begin. 'After I arrived in Manchester.

Before I left, Paul gave me money and an address.'

'Your Uncle Paul?' She interrupts.

'Yes, Da's brother. He gave me £200 and the address of a woman, Joan Kelly. He said she would have a room for me.'

Cathryn checks her notes. 'You and your father had been living with your uncle and his wife?'

I tell her about Uncle Paul and Josie. 'I frightened her, I think.'

'Why?'

I shrug. 'I was a teenager, I had bad dreams, I was … intense.'

'Did you argue with her?'

'No, never.' I shake my head. 'We were just … we were never a family. Paul had worked abroad for years, he met and married Josie in Australia. By the time they came back to the village I was ten years old, and we didn't have' — I search for the right words — 'shared experiences … memories. The things that connect families. It was different for Paul, he grew up with Da, and I suppose he saw a younger Da in both me and Maria. But we were strangers to Josie, and we were unruly kids. Before Ma and Maria … ' I falter. 'We never became close and then, I was living in her house. I don't blame her, not at all.'

'So, you went to Manchester and found work?'

The sofa is absorbing the heat of the sun, but the top of my neck feels raw, my back hot and itchy. I think about the day I left, the crossing, not knowing where I was going or what I'd find when I got there. An image of my hands on the rail of the ferry, clenched, knuckles white, looking back towards everything that I was running from. I was tall by then, and already shaving twice a day. But though I looked like a man, those hands belonged to a boy.

I remember the wind, the tears streaming down my face, tasting the salt splashing up from the churning ocean. The excitement and fear, like electricity in my groin. Glad to be leaving, but homesick before Dublin disappeared.

I return to the question Cathryn asked; she wants everything in sequence.

'Yes, I went by ferry, then caught the train from Holyhead to Manchester. It felt alien, the look of the houses, the roads, even the fields. The train was hot with the sun streaming in the windows though it was still early. I was hungry and went to the dining car. Paul had given me money, and I had some of my own that I'd saved; I felt rich — proud to be looking after myself in a strange country. I ordered a breakfast, but it tasted awful. The sausages were bland and hard to cut, the rashers were glistening with salt. Everything was different, but it was the small things — flavours, smells and tastes that hit me hardest. The tea was insipid, and when I put milk into the cup it turned almost full white. I'd never seen a tea bag with a string attached to it! I tried to stir the tea, and the bag knotted around the spoon.' I pause, remembering the sense of strangeness, my fingers trying to untangle it, trembling.

'The journey took a few hours and when I arrived in the city, I had to ask for directions to Joan Kelly's house. Paul knew her from his own time working there; he told me she'd look after me. He was right.' I smiled, remembering Joan and the way she welcomed me.

'Arriving in her house was like coming home,' I say.

'She was a big woman, all smiles and laughter. She was kind. Joan rented rooms to engineers and office workers, shop girls and stevedores, all of them Irish. She knew all the Irish in the city, all the shops, the bars and restaurants. It was her who found me the job in the Anvil and Forge. Joan never realised … '

'A pub.' Cathryn sat forward, taking notes.

'Yes, a pub and restaurant, just off Princess Road, close enough to the university. The landlord was an Irish man, Brian Kenny, the clientele a mix of local and students. I liked it… at first, anyway. It drew a young crowd and I was anonymous, and there was little chance of me bumping into anyone that knew me.

'But I was lonely in Manchester, a city full of Irish, first and second generation, with names like Boyle and O'Reilly and Gallagher, all claiming to be Irish in pure Mancunian. For a while I was a celebrity, my burr setting me apart, marking me as a genuine Paddy. Locals and students were eager to tell me their stories, about fathers from Cork or mothers from Galway. But that passed.

'As the locals got to know me, I became Paddy, or Irish; only Brian called me Dan.'

'You said you liked it at first. So, what changed?'

At first, I struggled to answer Cathryn's questions. The whole process seemed like an invasion, forcing me to revisit a history I wasn't proud of. But I realised this was her role, to listen, to interrupt me only to explore some point that she felt was important.

'First it was drink,' I said, skirting Abbey for now.

'I'd never been a drinker at home, and from the start Brian told me not to drink in the pub during opening hours. So, when a customer said, 'Have one yourself,' I put the money in a jar by the till, just like all the other lads did, and we'd split it at the end of the week.

'Most evenings I'd walk home straight after closing — back to my lodging. But there were nights I had to stay back to help, and after the cleanup, when it was just me and a few of the barmen and Brian Kenny, they'd have a beer. Some of the lads were real drinkers. I was young and competitive, and there was the social thing; I was living on my own, so Brian and the lads in the Forge were … family, I suppose. At first, I drank Coke, but later … ' I shrug. 'I saw no harm in it.'

Cathryn wrote more and I sat back, recalling those nights in the Forge. I can still taste the insipid English beer, and though I'd no experience of drinking, I had an Irishman's distaste for the sudsy and too warm ale. I drank it because the other lads did, and one beer became two and two became three and something was stirring and popping and fizzing in my blood.

'So, this was when you started to drink,' Cathryn prompts.

My laughter emerges as dry and humourless.

'I started and continued, I drank beer first, but I didn't like it, so I changed to whiskey. At the time, it'd been fine — I worked every day, I did my job, and I earned my pay. I drank on evenings I stayed back to clean up, then after a while I drank on the nights I was off-duty going to different bars or clubs. All the barmen in the city knew each other, we were a brotherhood, I suppose … I felt included. Back then, I never drank alone. Joan wouldn't allow it in the house, she was very Irish in that way. Her house, despite the endless rows of terraces that surrounded it, could have been lifted straight out of the village and transplanted there, complete with the picture of John Paul II and the Late Late Show on Friday nights and her pioneer pin.'

'But later?'

'Yes.' I look at her. 'Later it became a problem.' I stumble over the words, my leg aches and my head throbs from the coffee, wired and alert, but also distant, exhausted from the endless reliving of the past.

'Take your time.'

I look up at the clock: it's only 6.55 am. I want to give up, tell her I've had enough, that I need to stop for a while. But she'd made time for me, left her bed in the early morning, her husband, her daughter.

I grip the top of my thigh and tug; I feel the pain jolt me back.

'I became a functioning alcoholic.' I cough out the words, and Cathryn waits, clasping her hands like a child in prayer, fingers intertwined and chin perched on top.

'I did everything I needed to do. I got up every morning, I showered, worked, paid my rent, did my laundry. Within a year I was drinking a bottle of whiskey a day, sometimes two. In those days I was thin; I didn't eat enough, but I had boundless energy. I smuggled bottles into my room, decanted them into Coke tins and juice cartons, and hid them in the small fridge where I kept milk and bottled water.'

I look across at her and grimaced.

'I was just another pisshead, killing myself.'

'So what changed?'

And there it is, just like that.

Abbey

'Abigail Taylor.'

Cathryn sits back. 'Tell me about the first time you saw her.'

I close my eyes.

'She walked in and just like that, the world was full of sunshine and possibility.' I feel foolish saying it but there was no other way to describe how I felt.

'Abbey, in all the time I knew her, always paused at the threshold; she made an entrance and it might have seemed to some that she was waiting for the applause. But it wasn't like that at all. It wasn't even a conscious thing, she wasn't a poser or attention seeker. You could see it in her face, her expression. She wasn't looking inward, imagining how she looked, but outward at how wonderful everything in front of her appeared.'

I would see the same look on her face later at the Avenue des Champs-Élysées in Paris, or the Trevi Fountain in Rome, and the hundreds of more and less significant places we visited together. The look that said, there was nowhere else she would rather be, and no one else she would rather be with.

I visualise her standing there that first day, her shadow falling through the smoke-laden air and stretching across the red and green carpet, towards me, as though even then she knew.

'She was wearing a raffia gaucho hat, and her

dress was strapless, a flimsy summer thing, pinks and muted oranges and blues, and the sun seemed to shine, not through it, but from it. Her legs were bare and tanned above a pair of half-cut cowboy boots. She stood in the doorway and the light from outside painted a bright, glowing nimbus around her.'

I close my eyes, lost in the memory.

'Abbey.'

I breathe her name and my stomach lurches, my pulse quickens and suddenly my mouth is dry.

'Can I get some water?'

'Of course.' Cathryn doesn't call Tiffany this time, but goes herself, giving me a moment. I grope for the pills in my pocket and swallow two. There are only six left and I still have a week before I can get more.

I check the clock: it's 7:05 am — only ten minutes have passed since the last time I looked, and it feels like an hour.

*

'So, you left Manchester with Abbey?'

Cathryn is sitting beside me again, and has turned her chair to face me.

'Yes, but not straightaway. She planned to stay in the UK for a month. Abbey was travelling with a guy, Russ.'

That first time, Abbey had spent four days in Manchester. She'd already seen the south coast and spent a weekend in London. They intended Manchester as an overnight stop only, planning to leave the following day for Edinburgh. When she left the Forge that evening, I never expected to see her again.

'She told me later that she walked to the station with Russ intending to get the train and only decided at the last moment to let him go on alone. Russ had family in Scotland, so she made the excuse of not wanting to play gooseberry. That was a Friday, and she promised Russ she would catch the train to Edinburgh on Tuesday morning.'

I take another sip of water and feel the coolness wash over my tongue. I replace the glass on the table; the surface of the water vibrates, and I draw my hand back and clench it to stop shaking.

'She came straight to the Forge from the train station.'

'The pub?' Cathryn's eyes are half closed, and I see a darkness about them, a sadness, that I had not seen before.

'Yes. She was there, talking to Brian Kenny when I got in. I didn't see her until she called out, 'Hey Irish!' She had this way of smiling, her eyes like … an invitation. After that, she only ever called me 'Irish'.

'I worked Friday until closing, and Brian told me not to come back until Tuesday. I think he saw how I looked at Abbey and how she looked at me.

'That night, when we walked out of the Forge, Abbey linked my arm in hers, and we walked for hours. We talked, or at least she did; I listened. She told me about growing up in Cape Town. We walked along the banks of the Tame and the sun was coming up behind the bridge when she kissed me for the first time.'

I clench my fist; I need another sip of water but

am not sure if I can reach for and lift the glass.

'That was the first night in over a year that I didn't drink. She stayed with me for two more nights.'

I feel a crooked smile crease my face and fear it will look like a grimace.

'Joan liked her, and allowed me to break the rules. By the time I walked Abbey to the train on Tuesday, I'd been dry for over four days. And it had been easy. I never needed to drink when she was with me, I never felt the compulsion. It was like she became my addiction.'

'And when she left?' Cathryn is rubbing a hand across her forehead.

'Are you ok?' I ask.

She looks at me and smiles. 'Yes, I'm fine. Just a little tired, I had a late night. Sorry, go ahead.'

'When she left, I was fine. She'd be in Scotland for less than two weeks and when she came back, I would join her and Russ, and we would go to Paris first, then Milan and then Rome. We'd planned it, and I had money saved, but I wanted to gather up as much as I could. I didn't drink for those twelve days, I ate only in the pub.

'I'd always been frugal, and despite what I blew on drink, I'd spent very little since I'd arrived in Manchester. When I went out, it was to bars where I knew the staff, or where the locals bought me drinks. I'd been in Manchester two years and I had £3000 pounds saved. When I left the station after dropping her off, I went straight to see Brian and handed in my notice. He was fine about it, and I promised him I'd work right up to the last night before I left.

I remember him shaking my hand and wishing me luck. Brian was a good skin, very Irish in lots of ways, but soft. He liked to see people getting on, and when I told him I was leaving, he looked at me with big rheumy eyes.

"You're doing right," he said. "You're not cut out for this game."

'I realise now that he was warning me. I think he saw himself in me, his younger self. He'd immersed himself in the life, drinking, and his face showed it, and his gut. He never found a way out, but he thought I had.'

'Ok, let's leave that for now.'

I look at Cathryn, her eyes are full of empathy.

'Let's take ten minutes.'

I stay on the couch and she goes out to talk to Tiffany.

Trapped

In the beginning, Cathryn focused on the circumstances of my life. For a week we spoke about addiction and recovery. Today is the first time she's probing, forcing me to pick away at scabs. And I haven't broken down, cried in front of her or raged at her. I find it easy to speak to her, to look into her eyes and tell her truths I had up until now admitted only to myself.

I sit on the couch, staring at the window, seeing the clouds that drift past but not registering them. Waiting for Cathryn.

*

'The Lady in the Glass. Who is she?'

And I am back in the village, standing in front of the house, thinking about a day thirty years earlier.

In sober moments I believe that at the centre of the cosmos is a pulse, a steady beat, the sound of stories unfolding, of lives and hearts in sync, chaos inhaled, and history exhaled.

The Lady in the Glass, who is she? A grandmother, an ageing aunt, some distant relative come to watch over a child? The sight of her pulled me up. Can others see her, or is she only there for me?

She was born whole, came into being on a day of storms, on a day when we stoked fires and shivered.

She is an image in a shattered pane of glass.

But I don't say that; it would sound contrived.

'She's an image, an optical illusion.'

'Tell me.' There is an insistence to Cathryn's tone.

'I'll tell you how she came to be,' I say, and she nods. She has abandoned her notepad; her pen lies untouched on the coffee table and she is leaning towards me.

I close my eyes and recall a cold morning. I had been looking down at the room below; it was bright at the centre and the fire glowed, but at the edges it was dark and cold.

'The stairs were narrow and bare, the bannister rails close together, and I was sitting in the dark looking down.'

'How old were you?'

'Fourteen, and Maria was sixteen.'

'So it was that year?'

I nod.

'Ok, go ahead.'

'It's cold — it's March. Ma was sitting at the fireplace with Bridget O'Connor. I remember Bridget sitting so close to the fire that her legs had gone red.'

'Who was Bridget O'Connor?'

'A widow, her house was close to the crossroads. She lived with an ageing brother, looked after him, though she was not much younger than him. She kept to herself, aloof — thought herself a cut above the rest of the villagers. Ma called her a failed nun; it was an opinion shared by others. The locals called her nosy, a gossip.

'She came to buy eggs from Ma every Monday. That day, Ma invited her to stay and have a cup of tea. I fled to the top of the narrow stairs and sat there,

78

out of sight .'

'Why did you flee?'

I consider this.

'Ma didn't like Bridget. I think she hated her, but she would do anything to impress her.' I feel my face twist into a frown. 'But she never would.'

'Impress her?'

I nod. 'Our house was dark and cold. And we — Maria, Da and I — were a disappointment that Ma wore like a yoke. She tried to be something she wasn't and we … Maria and I, knew from the start that it would end badly.'

'What happened?'

'I returned to the bannisters, and looked down. The orange glow was shrinking, and the darkness was pulling in closer. Ma and Bridget sat surrounded by it.

'Ma was in … an expansive humour, she'd been drinking. She'd changed by then — was drinking most days, her face was flushed, and though she couldn't see it, I could — Bridget O'Connor, reeling back from the stink of Ma's whiskey breath every time she leaned forward to say something.'

I picture the scene again, the darkness gathering, closing in about the hearth.

'She sat across the fire from Bridget, talking. I heard low murmurs. Maria was in the kitchen, I heard water being poured into a kettle and crockery rattling as she took cups and saucers down off the high shelves — the good china, with pink roses and vines of green thorn … '.

I close my eyes, searching my memory for the

other details, the things that happened before.

'Maria was scalding the teapot — I could hear the splash of the hot water into the ceramic sink. Then she filled it, the aroma wafting from the scullery.'

'So Maria was making tea?' Cathryn clarifies, gently.

'Yes.'

She nods and closes her eyes.

'Maria appeared with the tray. I saw her stepping on the bloodstone that separated the back kitchen from the living room, and the single step down into the front room. She was carrying a tray with the china pot, two cups and a sponge cake on a clean tea-towel, and a black-handled knife with a long wide blade balanced on the edge. Maria set it down and Ma reached forward and cut two wedges of cake while Maria poured the tea.'

I recall the way Bridget watched Maria, her eyes predatory.

'Bridget spoke, her voice louder. "You've grown up so quick!" Her sharp eyes flashed over the bruise on Maria's cheek, taking in her thin frame.

'Maria's hand shook as she lifted the milk jug. I knew she wanted Bridget to shut up.

'Ma scowled, looking at Maria. "That's fine," she said. "We can look after ourselves."

'I saw the relief in Maria's eyes, but Bridget spoke again. "Did you fall?" She was sipping her tea, pretending to ask an innocent question, but she knew, she fucking knew, like everyone else knew. She could have kept her mouth shut, she should have, but she didn't.

'Ma and Maria spoke, their words merging.

"I … was helping Da," began Maria.

"She knocked into the clothesline," Ma cut across her. "She's very careless sometimes." Her eyes hardened; she knew that Bridget understood.

'I saw the blood drain from Maria's face. Ma's voice changed, the tone rising.

'Bridget O'Connor nodded but she wouldn't take her eyes off Maria's cheek.

"Go on up to your brother and make sure he has his homework done," Ma said, pretending nothing had happened. But her voice betrayed her, that rising inflection, like a tree swaying and creaking before a gathering storm.

'Maria ran up the stairs, passed me. I felt her touch my shoulder, and I looked down at Ma. I watched as she ate a thin slice of sponge cake, her eyes intent on something Bridget said, as though nothing had happened The darkness closed all around them, the fire a pinprick at the centre. I stood, and followed Maria into the loft, our space, the space Ma never entered.'

I pause, thinking about that morning, my jaw clamping, wanting to hide but Cathryn is waiting.

'Maria was a year and a half older than me. I was a tall fourteen and she a petite sixteen, and even then I was taller than her. But you couldn't measure the differences between us in the sum of our heights or ages.

"I fucking hate her!" Maria sat on her bed.

"Me too." I sat beside her, wanting to swear as Maria had, searching for a word that would be equal to the contempt I felt for Ma. It was cold, our breath was steaming, the heat rising from below and meeting the chill that descended from above.

"What are you going to do?" I asked.

"What is there to do?" Maria looked at me and I saw she was crying, tears of resignation and frustration.

*

'Ma didn't always act straightaway. Sometimes she waited, and those were often the worst times. But that day her fury came unrestrained. We froze to the sound of crockery being reorganized, Bridget's voice calling goodbye, and the front door closing. We sat in silence, waiting.

'Ma called Maria, her voice tight and angry.

'Again, I sidled to the bannister and sat with my face poking between the rails. I stayed there, frozen — afraid of Ma, of her temper, and what she might do.

'Maria never showed her fear. She wasn't brazen, or disrespectful, just unresponsive. She absorbed it all and gave nothing back. It was a long time before I understood that she accepted it so Ma would aim her temper at her and not me.'

My voice catches at this last, I feel the anger and shame like a fist clenching in my chest.

'Your mother beat her?'

I shrug at the question.

I've told Cathryn about the beating, the screaming and kicking, the nails that slashed like talons, the teeth biting. But this is the first time she has asked me to describe a specific incident.

The Lady in the Glass

I don't want this to define our lives; I don't want abuse to become an excuse. We were more than the sum of our experience — we had our own minds, our own free will. But this time Cathryn asks: two words that insist on clarity.

'Tell me.'

And so I do.

*

'Ma stood with her hands on her hips and Maria stood in front of her, back very straight, eyes steady, not accusing but not frightened either.

"You're after making a holy fucking show of me," Ma hissed. "What sort of fool are you, saying that in front of that old bitch?" Her voice rose an octave, but Maria stood still.

"Well! What have you to say for yourself?" Still Maria stayed quiet, and I continued whispering. "Say something, say something!"

Ma balled her hand into a fist, but Maria didn't flinch.

"Say something!" I repeated. My lips moved, but no sound came out

'Ma's fist rose, knuckles clenched, bone white and hard like a rock. She punched, and Maria's head shot back. The only sound was Ma's breathing.'

I stop for a minute and wipe my hand across my mouth.

'A tiny drop of blood landed on the curtains that screened the room from the outside world.

"How dare you?" Ma screamed. I clung tighter to the rails, my lips still moving.

"Say something, say something, say something!"

'But Maria only moved when Ma's hand went to the knife on the tray. She stepped back, knocking the table. Cups toppled and crashed on the grey flagstones and Ma's fist curled around the black handle of the knife, and … I don't remember standing, just my feet already on the stairs, terrified that she would really hurt her this time.

'But Maria stood up to Ma; even with a knife held to her chest, she showed no fear. It was only when I pushed Ma away that Maria saw me. Her eyes widened, her mouth forming an "Oh", and she grabbed my arm, dragging me towards the door, wrapping herself around me, with Ma screaming behind us. Then I heard something breaking.

'A hole appeared in the door glass, fragments flew outward, and I thought Ma had thrown a cup or a plate at it. Maria pushed the door, propelling me out into the freezing cold. I'd no shoes on and the ground was still white with frost, but I didn't care, I wanted to get away. Maria slammed the door behind her, more glass fell; she pushed me ahead and we ran towards the yard.

'I saw the knife — buried to the handle in the icy ground, and behind us Ma was still screaming. Maria was strong, she shoved me past the feather-house and the machine shed, out into the yard where Da was running towards us.

"What happened?" His face was pale and his eyes burned. 'Maria stopped running and grabbed me, hugging me tight, screaming at Da, not afraid, but indignant.

"She threw a fucking knife at us!' she cried. 'She could have killed him!' Maria hugged me close.

Da sent us to the barn. His face was contorted with grief, or anger. "Go on, I'll quieten her," he said. "Don't come in until I call you."

*

'Later, Da called us in for breakfast. Ma sat at the table, her face emotionless. She glanced at Maria but didn't acknowledge the bruises or the blood under her nose; she never acknowledged the damage she inflicted.

'I sat at the table, but the food tasted like ash. I couldn't look at Ma, afraid she would see the loathing in my eyes.

'Maria stared at the food on the table and left, never once looking at Ma or Da. I followed her to the barn. She sat on the rail that enclosed the six pigs, already big enough to slaughter. I approached with caution; I thought she'd be angry with me. But I don't think she even saw me. She sat with her hands deep in her jacket pockets, her head forward, her hair falling over her face — she made a sound like an injured animal.

"Are you ok?"

She looked at me and tears were streaming down her bruised and bloody face.

"I fucking hate her, Danny! She's a fucking bitch, I wish she was dead."

'I nodded, because I wished the same thing.

'I never wished she'd be different because I knew it wasn't possible, but I wished she was dead, gone, out of our lives.

'Then one day, she left, and Maria too. And I was alone and unanchored.'

*

Cathryn still doesn't understand, how can she? So I tell her how Da repaired the glass in the door by placing a second sheet behind the original one, and another in front. He preserved the broken glass in the way a dried flower might be preserved. He never said whether he did it to remind Ma what she had done, or for some other reason, but the shape of the broken glass remained and, as small pieces dropped away, The Lady in the Glass emerged, her shape growing into that of a woman with a bonnet, wide skirts. The Lady in the Glass, an encased pane, cracked but not broken, splinter lines and strata shaped in random patterns that to a child's eye, an eye that sought order, became an old-fashioned lady. The Lady in the Glass, Keeper of the Door, the sentinel at the entrance to our home.

'Was she kind-hearted?' Cathryn asks.

I look at her, unsure if her question is serious, or if she is mocking me.

'Perhaps I endowed her with kind-heartedness,' I reply. 'It is only I who see her, I never shared her with Maria, or anyone else. She became my … talisman.'

*

I return to the bareness, the long shadows, the trees looming over the house. And the Lady in the Glass, my first view of the house. She still stood guard at the door, unchanged after thirty years. A filigree of green stains her etched outline where moss and algae had filled the deeper parts of her tracery but otherwise she is unaltered.

That cracked glass in the front door confronts me and makes me hesitate, my breath catching at that place where screams form. I am a boy again on the cusp of terror; the image in the glass brings a jolt, a concrete connection. A link to a mother, father and sister. Beyond her monsters gather, and there on the threshold I brace myself. I have a choice; I can still turn back. Or, I can go on — confront the dragon and kill it, let it wash out of me. I reach forward and push.

The glass and its improbable icon had fared better than the splintered door with its peeling, blistered paint and damp-stained panels. It hangs like a drunk, the top hinge collapsing inward, the lower one tottering. I hesitate there on the threshold, terrified. Am I ready to face what waits for me beyond The Lady in the Glass? Prepared to scratch at the scabs that had formed over this pile of stone? I have stocked and stored its days, screened them away, place them in the darkness. Now I will draw them out again. The diggers would come soon; later would be too late.

Like betrayal

As I leave Cathryn's office, I notice a man lounging against Tiffany's desk, speaking to her and laughing loudly. He seems out of place, not a client. After seven days, I can recognise clients — the dark-rimmed eyes and furtive, defensive posture as they clutch their pain close. I've categorised them — the deniers, who believe they are fine; the conquered, who believe they will never be fine again; and the chancers, who think they're gaming the system. I know it's cruel, but it's a self-aimed cruelty, and I wonder which I am.

This man is none of these things. He's tall, six-three, or six-four. Broad, but not in the overall way of a working man; he's a boxer or a rugby player, I guess — his back straight and arms filling his sleeves, biceps defined through the loose material. There's a restrained arrogance and aggressiveness about him. His hair is foppish, too boyish for a man I guess to be about forty — tight on the sides and over long on top, falling over his face. It's blond, almost white, and coloured, I'm sure. His face sports trimmed stubble, darker, with hints of grey.

As I call goodbye to Tiffany, he glances at me. His eyes hold none of the timidity of Cathryn's clients; they're bright and inquisitive. My reaction is visceral, an immediate dislike. There's something familiar about him, but I can't say what it is.

I take the stairs, balancing on the crutch and shuffling, one step at a time, twisting sideways to compensate for the pain. I'm glad not to meet anyone on my way down as I'm wrung out, my mind numb. But I consider the progress made. Recounting my visit to the house and responding to Cathryn's questions had revealed much more than my visit alone. I wonder how much pain it might cause.

*

Outside, the sun has risen clear of the buildings, and now hides behind high cloud. The day will be close and humid. Late August is true to form; Dublin looks drab, the exuberance of summer is past and autumn has yet to arrive. The city hangs in that mid-period, with a languid acceptance of lassitude which mirrors my humour.

The street is busy. Cars and buses move past, the air is full of the stink of exhaust and the sounds of traffic, blaring horns, and the din of commuters.

Across from me, on the shaded side of the street, is a café. Just visible through the rushing traffic, its windows are square segments reflecting the moving cars, while everything behind them is dark. I hobble across at the traffic lights, negotiating my way through the tightly packed vehicles, drivers impatiently tapping their steering wheels. I gain the far pavement and limp to the entrance.

Inside, the café is dim, wall-lights painting warm pools over vacant tables. There's a queue at the counter — office workers, ordering coffee to go. I sit down at a table, the pain in my hip a low dull ache.

A waitress drops a newspaper on the table.

'Be with you in a moment, love.'

*

I open the paper. The headlines are a predictable mix of austerity, homelessness, water charges and protests. I am an avid reader of news, though I form no strong opinions; I dislike the emotional, reactionary journalistic slant. I am a centrist, with a left leaning; I see the reasons for some measures that the populists decry, yet I empathise with the working man who shouts foul when the government raids his meagre wage packet. But this morning the unfolding drama of modern Ireland holds no interest for me.

I watch the moving traffic and people hurrying past, all destined for desks in the bustling city. I feel removed from it all, waiting for something to finish, and something new to begin.

Since starting to see Cathryn, I am eager to face the past, not so I can wallow in it or forget it, but so that I might move past it. But at the house, I missed whatever I should have noticed, the image or memory that Maria insists I recall.

*

When I met Cathryn for the first time, she asked me, other than reuniting with Maria, what I hoped to achieve. I'd found it hard to answer without using clichés such as 'closure' or 'forgiveness.' But I knew what I wanted — to face my guilt, take responsibility for the things I'd done, and prove that I wasn't predestined to be an addict or a partner who runs from confrontation. Because if I don't accept my portion of blame, then I might as well cede all control over my life.

My mind is full of these things — the interior of a forgotten house, a brave sister, and Abbey, whom I last saw in a student house in Exeter — when I glance out the window again, the man who had been flirting with Tiffany is leaving Cathryn's building, but he's not alone. Cathryn is walking behind him. As he turns towards her, he grasps her arm and she looks at him; I can't see her eyes, but her expression is annoyed. They walk down the street together, with a distance between them that seems fraught.

*

The phone vibrates in my pocket; the screen shows Maria's number.

'How was it?' she asks.

'Fine,' I answer, and exhale. 'Hard. But I survived.'

'How was Cathryn?'

'She's good … she looked a little tired, as though she has something on her mind, but she's good, she's great.' And I realise I mean it.

'Yes, she is.'

Though I can't see it, I can sense her smile.

'Can we meet?'

'Soon.' There is regret in her tone, but resolve too.

'Ok … I'm sorry, I understand,' I say, trying to mean it.

'Chat later.'

'Wait!' I say. 'I have a question. Cathryn is married, right?'

There's a pause, and I imagine her pinching her lip.

'It's only curiosity.'

'Yes, she's married — to Michael Grant.' Now I know why I recognised him.

'The newsreader?'

'I'm working, Danny — I have to go. I'll call you later.' The phone goes dead.

The waitress comes and stands beside me.

'What can I get for you?' I look up at her. For a moment I've forgotten where I am.

'Sorry … I'll just have a coffee to go.'

She looks at the crutch and nods as though in understanding.

*

I'd seen the article; it was a gossip piece in a Sunday supplement. I want to read it again, so I spend €18 on a cab back to the studio.

It's still on the breakfast bar; I'm not the tidiest of people. Not that I'm slovenly — I don't like dirt — but I accept the detritus of living. I retain the habits I first adopted in Joan's house in Manchester. Every morning I squeeze my narrow frame into the walk-in shower, I change my underwear every day, and I never wear the same thing for over two days. I take my clothes to the laundromat on Tuesdays and Thursdays, and on Saturdays I strip the bed and haul the sheet and duvet to the same laundromat in bin liners. But in other ways, I'm untidy. I wash my few dishes every morning after breakfast and every evening after dinner, but I don't always dry them, or put them away. My jacket hangs over the back of my single chair more often than on the hook behind the door. My coffee table strains under the weight of books that I intend to return to the library. I clutter the breakfast bar with keys and loose change, and my fruit bowl today contains leaflets, a baseball cap, sunglasses, an empty pill box — and the magazine.

He is on a side panel of the front cover, shoulder pierced with a staple. I recognise the photo; it had announced his appointment: 'The New Voice of News on STV.'

The picture shows him in a white suit, arms folded and piercing eyes turned towards the camera. A blond woman, his fellow presenter, stands to his right, her hand on his shoulder, legs crossed coquettishly, pouting — reminiscent of a Bond poster.

The box below contains a headline:

WHAT'S GOING ON
WITH STV'S NEWS TEAM?

.STV's new front man, Michael Grant, and his glamorous fellow presenter, Alissa Bale, caused quite a stir when they were photographed together in Longman's, the popular nightspot in Chelsea, after their appearance together at the ITR awards in London just a week ago. Grant, who lives in Wicklow, bought a house in Leeds recently. Alissa Bale (28) is the long-time partner of well-known businessman Hugh Gordon. The couple have two children. Grant is also married …

*

I stop reading, feeling that I've invaded Cathryn's privacy and been disloyal to her. I toss the magazine into the bin. Her life is none of my concern, yet I cannot shake the feeling that I've betrayed her.

My next appointment is not until Saturday morning.

Kin

Before the killing, we were a family, conflicted, dysfunctional, begotten of our own history, a tangle of blood and sex and longing.

The village was a community united by rebellion and divided by old enmities. Some families bore the shame of being friends of the Tans and others we lauded as scions of rebels. We clung to some people and ostracised others. Maria called it The Tangle Box, or the roots of our evil.

*

Da came from an old village family; the first of them arrived during the famine years. A headstone at the foot of a ruined stone church in a field on a hill above the village shows the names of four generations of O'Neill.

Thomas and Paul O'Neill were the only surviving children of Thomas O'Neill and Agnes Ellis. Both my grandparents came from village stock, Agnes's family arriving a generation after Thomas's. They were subsistence farmers, considered well-to-do. Agnes's father attended sodality, was a staunch Catholic, and supplemented his farming income as a grave keeper, not only digging the graves but also tending the graveyard of the now ruined church.

Thomas's family were mariners. A plaque on the harbour wall commemorates the death of Da's brothers, William O'Neill (23) and George O'Neill

(26) lost off the ketch Molly in 1949. The O'Neills were, to a man, merchant seamen or fishermen.

Da and Paul both became fishermen; neither of them envisaged any other life. But Paul, who had left the village years before, travelling first to England and later to Australia, only returned when his father died, inheriting the house on the harbour and the boat, a twenty-foot crabber also called Molly.

Da inherited the farm which had been in Agnes's family for three generations, ten acres of rough pasture, a yard of stone-built buildings and a house originally constructed of straw and daub, which he later reinforced with hand cast concrete bricks made in forms.

*

Agnes's will created a division between the brothers. As the eldest, Da felt entitled to the family house on the harbour and the boat, but instead became an unwilling, and bad, farmer. He had no love for or connection to the land. He worked the small farm in the same way as Agnes's father had worked it — he didn't modernise or expand it, but practised subsistence farming long after it became unviable.

While Paul was absent, Da fished with his father, but after he became too weak to go to sea, Agnes forbid Da to take the Molly out alone; she lay in the harbour unused, mocking him daily. Agnes's spite marked Da in a way few understood.

But that grudge didn't extend to Paul. Da accepted his lot in the manner of a man born to acceptance; he saw nothing deficient in his life. Poverty sat lightly on his shoulders; he made do and saw it as a virtue. The villagers liked him; he was a mass-goer, a contented man. His only deviance was his love of rugby, an English game, but by 1968, when he travelled to London to see Ireland play in Twickenham, even that oddity was unremarkable. It was when he returned, later than expected, with Caroline Caulk on his arm, that tongues began to wag.

*

The village people considered us comfortable; we had land but, despite appearances, we were never much above poor. While Da may not have been bitter about his lot, he never embraced it either, eyeing the land, farm, and decaying buildings with acrimony. The two fields that sat between him and the sea he yearned for were a cross he bore.

He kept suckler cows, fed pigs on waste, and cultivated a large garden where he grew potatoes and vegetables, apples and pears. Each year, one offspring of the small suckler herd made its way to the freezer in the scullery. The meat of one pig was also cached there, the remaining stock sold with eggs and foul; the combined kitty provided the little disposable income we had. We never went hungry, we had meat and when Da worked with Paul on the Mary J we had fish; we were never short of potatoes, fruit or vegetables, but we had little extra money.

*

Maria was born in 1970, I followed in 1972. Born into a way of life, I make no excuses for; I blame my parents for what we suffered, but try to understand the cause. When you're a child, you believe you deserve the things you experience, the good and the bad. But as I grew older, I understood that no child deserves neglect or mistreatment.

So, I became a collector of our history; I assembled the pieces, the fragments of information delivered in Da's soft voice or in Ma's harsh one. I have been the curator of words and images and have moulded them into shapes; I cannot say that they are all factual, but they are real to me.

The story of Ma's first encounter with the village set the tone for her life. It disappointed her, and her disappointment would turn to bitterness. Part of the story came from Da, on a night when he comforted me. My back was bleeding and my chest was tight.

I related the story to Cathryn during the first week.

*

'Don't hate her, Danny.'

His eyes were bleary, distant. I nodded because he seemed so sad.

'She's mardered with grief.' He said. 'And disappointment. But she wasn't always like that. I suppose it was me that let her down.'

Da told me then, how they'd met in 1968, when she was thirty-two and he was thirty-four.

'She had no family, Danny, no mother or father. She worked as a waitress in a pub in Twickenham. I'd come to London for a big match, Ireland against England.' He smiled, but not at me; he was so immersed in the memory I might as well not have been there.

'Neither of us knew much, we were so unprepared.' He spoke as though they were love-struck teens.

Agnes, who hated Caroline, told me before she

died how 'the bride' got drunk and passed out at the wedding.

But there were two sides to that story. I visualise it the way Ma told it, from memory, and the things she revealed in temper. I imagine the village as it looked when the newly married couple returned after their honeymoon. How her disappointment began.

*

Tommy turned the white Ford Cortina at the corner and drove down a road that was barely a track. It was April 1968, and the sun was warm. Tommy looked handsome, tanned from the sun of Bretagne, and Caroline felt relaxed and happy. She hadn't told Tommy yet that she was pregnant.

Small houses hugged the curb, and between them were open spaces, grass fields that stretched to the hedging, and Caroline felt lost in the openness, she already missed the life and vibrancy of the city but looked forward to seeing the house which Tommy had described to her. They entered the lane and when Caroline saw the house for the first time, she sat up straight, her eyes narrowed, and her mouth tightened.

The house was so small, with a glass porch that looked as if it might fall at the least breath of wind running along its front, and the latch on the front dripped with rust. Tommy worked the key and pushed the door inwards; it snagged on a groove in the work-worn linoleum. She entered a single room, in shock, and didn't notice a second doorway that led to a dark hallway, seeing only how small it all was.

The house smelled of must and mildew. She placed her hand on a wall to steady herself, then pulled it away in alarm; the bare plaster was greasy with dampness.

Tommy dropped the cases he'd carried from the car and showed her the kitchen where there was a sink, a gas ring and a table with a dirty red oilcloth tacked to its greasy surface. She sat down on a wooden seat, one of a pair, and put her head in her hands to stifle a sob. Tommy placed a hand on her arm, and she shrugged it off before standing and squaring her shoulders.

'Is there hot water?' she asked. Tommy shook his head. She found a large pot in the only cupboard in the kitchen, filled it with water and places it on the ring to boil. Tommy disappeared, and the sound of the door closing grated on her nerves.

On the sink she found rags, most of which she dumped into a potato sack that lay by the back door. She salvaged two, and once the water had boiled, she set about cleaning.

Later, she felt faint and sat on the sofa that she had scrubbed over and over until the colour of its upholstery became visible. The pain of disappointment washed through her.

Later still, when Tommy came in, she had peeled potatoes and prepared a stew.

The first time she cried was when the baby miscarried. She would cry again, many times, through bouts of disappointment, resentment and later hate. Ma would lose two more babies, but those would be different.

By the time Maria arrived in 1970, Ma had no more tears left. She'd closed in on herself, hardened and coalesced. The blood of a father she had no memory of fizzed and popped in her veins, and she was already drinking secretly.

The Tangle Box

I climb the stairs, and this time it is easier. There are few people in the city this early on a Saturday. The building resonates with emptiness, the sound of power humming through lines, the click of a phone switchboard, the cables of a nearby elevator .

Tiffany is not at the front desk. The door to Cathryn's office is ajar and I hear her moving about.

'Come in, Dan,' she calls. 'We're all alone today.'

She is arranging files on a shelf, and as she turns to greet me, I am struck by her appearance. She is wearing casual clothes, faded blue jeans and a man's shirt, large on her, unbuttoned with a tee-shirt with a glittery design underneath. Her face is shining, and though I am sure she is wearing makeup, I cannot detect it. She looks girlish, vulnerable; I pause for a minute, looking at her.

'Wow!' I smile. 'Who knew that beneath that professional exterior … '

She blushes, and I am immediately contrite.

'I mean … you're different, good different.'

'I'm picking my daughter up from dance classes later, we're going to a movie, so I'm on a tight schedule and didn't think I would have time to change.'

I know that she considered carefully how to present herself, and I'm glad that she shows this side of her person. But I just nod. 'You look nice.'

'How's your leg today?'

'Better, it's healing. I can walk without the crutch, but I still carry it. I like the image, the wounded vulnerability thing suits me.'

'It does!' She regains the initiative and now it's my turn to feel awkward.

She checks her watch and I stare at the clock. It's 8.15 am.

'Ok, let's make a start.'

*

Cathryn takes a seat and I drop into the one opposite and wait.

My folder is in front of her. It has grown over the preceding weeks, and now contains not only Cathryn's copious notes, but my medical records, the details of my self-sustained injuries, and my attempts at … I halt the thought.

She is flicking through it.

'Let's go back to the house.' She looks up. 'How did it feel to be there?'

'Frightening,' I answer. 'To tell the truth, it terrified me. I was thinking about Maria, wishing that she was beside me, holding my hand. She was braver than me. She had this … ability to read everything, her eyes alert, her arms around me, hugging me, busy constructing … walls around us both.'

'You were very close to her?'

'She was my sister, so yes. But she was more than that.'

'How so?'

I hunch my shoulders and exhale. 'She was a friend, and sometimes a parent too. She was only sixteen when … '

I can't finish the sentence and for the first time that week the immensity of it all closes in on me. I want to stand up, to pace. Instead, I grit my teeth and breathe. And then it passes.

'She called it The Tangle Box. As if it were a game or a puzzle, something we could find our way out of. And I was entering The Tangle Box again, only this time I didn't have her to guide me.'

'You were alone,' Cathryn states, rather than asks.

When I agreed to see her, I expected empathy, or sympathy. Someone who would understand me, comfort me, and tell me it was ok to be me. But she'd only ever pointed me towards myself, then let me talk, prompting when it was appropriate. And I was learning that the journey was mine; there could be empathy, but no sympathy, just a beginning and an ending.

'You entered the house?'

'Yes. I stood for the longest time at the threshold, then I pushed the door open, the rusted hinges screeching. Dust and cobwebs dispersed in a grey cloud, and in front of me was the front room.'

I close my eyes and allow the images to come.

'The dining table had collapsed, the veneer buckled and cracked. It sat askew on its three remaining legs. I was surprised. It looked smaller, but then, my memories were those of a child.'

I open my eyes and shrug.

'Doesn't everything diminish over time?' I asked. 'Don't all the things we once thought large become insignificant as we grow older?'

'Do you believe that's true?' She is intent, and her question has a weight that I recognise.

'No. Not all things diminish,' I answer gruffly. I swallow. 'Some form carbuncles — they grow and fester and take up the largest, most important part of you.'

I know those wounds, the ones that will not heal, but wrap you in layer after layer of loathing.

My voice grows louder. 'Things that can drive you to the edge of a roof over a city, that can send you plunging to ...' I choke on the words.

'What, Dan? Send you plunging to what?' She is relentless, her eyes compelling.

'To this ... or to a dead house.'

She gives me a moment. My hands tremble and my pulse quickens, but I'm ready to go on.

'My chair — the one that faced the window — was missing. Maria's chair — the one that faced mine — was still there, but in a different place, holding up the table at one sides. Dust and straw and bird shit covered the floor.'

*

I picture the room as it once was, remembering how we sat to eat but I have no clear memory of Maria sitting on her chair; it was hers only by default. The other three chairs had owners: Da and Ma who sat at either side of the table, facing each other, Ma closest to the kitchen, Da closer to the front door, while I faced the window, looking out over the yard, the barn, the block and tackle and swinging chains.

Maria hovered, invisible, pushing herself to the periphery of our family. She served, cleared and

104

cleaned, but her movements were so smooth that she barely disturbed the air, and even her breath was soft.

Out of sight of Ma, Maria's actions were quick and covert. She ate in the scullery, sometimes with a book balanced on her knee, the sound of water running slowly into a basin, ear cocked to the front room, listening, watchful. Ready to jump up and move to the sink, to wash and stack dishes.

She carried books, either stuffed into the back pocket of her jeans, or in her apron. She read in the nocks and crannies of the house that she claimed as her own, always ready to move if anyone approached.

*

Cathryn's voice cuts across the memory.

'What else was in the room?'

'Dust, and cobwebs … chips of plaster and paint that had fallen from the walls and ceiling. There had been other things there before, but they were gone, taken by whoever took the chair, maybe.'

In the centre I had found something I recognised — a gilded frame face down on the floor, the black cardboard stand damp and frayed. I picked it up and turned it over. It was water-stained behind the shattered glass. A photo. All four of us — Ma first, then Maria, Da and lastly me, all standing close together in a sea of bleached grass stubble and, behind us, bales of hay in stacks. Further back, the sea was a grey green bruise. I remove my wallet and take out the photograph, still folded between two €20 notes.

When I drew it from behind the shattered glass, it had felt fragile as if it might crumble in my hands. It has dried out now; the paper is crinkled and brittle, but the image is still clear. I stare at it before handing it to Cathryn.

Ma, Caroline O'Neill (née Caulk) is the tallest of us. She's thin, her sinewy arms poking from a short-sleeved, knee-length brown dress, and her legs are bare. It's late afternoon or early evening, the sun sinking behind whoever took the photograph. Ma is smiling but her grey eyes squint against the glare.

Maria is standing beside her, her sun-tanned, freckled arms folded. She's wearing blue jeans and a yellow tee-shirt, hair pulled back from her face. She is scowling, her eyes rejecting this pretence of happiness.

Da was a tiny man, but neat and meticulous. Even working, he looks almost dapper with turned-up trousers and boots that gleam. His body is small but wide and muscular, one hand leaning on the handle of a pitchfork. He's wearing braces, straps over his wide shoulders. His weather-beaten face is handsome, his mouth is twitching in a grin that might be sardonic, and his eyes are a dark, deep brown just like mine and Maria's.

I'm the last in line, standing with my hands by my sides. My dark brown hair is poking upward, skewed by a prominent calf's-lick, my ears are sticking out and my neck is long and thin. I'm wearing a blue tee-shirt with a collar. I'm grimacing at something.

Cathryn hands it back, pensively. 'Your mother was beautiful.'

I don't respond.

'When was it taken?'

I replace it in my wallet, wondering if anyone looking at the photograph now might predict the things to come. I am a month short of fourteen years old in the photograph, Maria has just turned sixteen. We will be a family for another ninety-eight days.

'It was the sixth of July, Maria's birthday. It was a Thursday.'

'That's very specific. You remember the day, why?'

'It was the day before Friday,' I grimace. 'Fridays were when Ma became "otherwise indisposed'

'What does that mean?'

'It was Maria who said it first,' I say.

Otherwise indisposed

'Explain the reference,' Cathryn says.

'Ma said illness was a weakness the poor could not afford. Being ill didn't excuse you from work. So, we were never sick.'

Cathryn nods. 'I'm with you so far.'

'Ma, up to that year, was never sick; she came from hardy stock. So when she drank, Maria would say she was "otherwise indisposed". I think she found it in a book, but I'm not sure. Ma was "otherwise indisposed" twice a month.'

'She was drunk, you mean?'

'No, not drunk — hung-over. It was a dangerous time, but a time of possibilities too.'

'Explain that.'

'When Ma drank, she changed. First, she became sweet, teasing us, telling us how much she loved us, telling us things would change, get better. "Sorry" became her favourite word. She spilled her heart onto the flagstones.

"I had no father or mother," she'd say. It always started the same way. That was the closest she'd ever come to acknowledging us.'

'Was there a trigger?' Cathryn asks.

'No. Nothing specific. Ma talked herself into fury — a name, a memory, and her voice would change, her bitterness and resentment would arise. Maria tried sometimes to deflect it.'

'How?'

'She'd try to keep Ma talking about the people she had loved, her grandmother or great-grandmother. "Tell us about Connie?" she'd whisper, her voice low and beguiling.

'Ma would shake her head. "She was the only one that gave a fuck."

'And we knew it was too late. Ma only swore when the dragon slithered to the surface — she changed, hardened, and her fists clenched.

'We learned to stay out of reach and avoid her touch, but we couldn't duck her words, words that reduced us to nothing. She told us how disappointed she was in us, called us stupid and useless.

'Later, when Ma had spent her fury, when she'd screamed and screeched, swore and cursed, and smashed things as though she could obliterate memories, then she'd fall silent.

'Later, Da would come and lift her from the chair in which she'd passed out. He'd put her to bed, and she'd sleep in the darkened room. And then, while she slept, we'd pretend to be normal.'

*

On those Friday nights, I learned the history of ourselves. Stories so often repeated, they became like stitches on my skin. And the people Ma spoke about — Connie and Ester — women who strove, whom we didn't know but learned to love, and Michael and William whom Ma despised.

Sometimes she spoke softly — she didn't see us when she was like that, she was in her own Elsewhere. She'd talk into the fire, her face flaccid, eyes distant, and rage held in abeyance. But we were veterans of Friday nights; we knew what would come, and that this was the opening act. We were at our most wary during this period of sweetness, because we knew that when it ended there'd be teeth and claws and tongues of fire.

*

I blink, and Cathryn gestures for me to continue.

'The hangover would last two days. Never more and never less. Four normal days and twenty-six crazy days per month. That was the metre of our lives, measured in steady allotments of crazy and sane, crazy and sane.'

'Was it always bad?' Cathryn asks as she writes in her notepad.

'No. Not at the start, anyway.'

Cathryn looks up, expectant.

'Ma drank whiskey.' I settle myself back into the chair. My leg wasn't bothering me at all this morning.

'She fooled herself that she had it under control, that she wasn't an alcoholic. But the pattern of her drinking was as predictable as that of any junkie.

'In the beginning, she didn't drink every day, she only drank on town days, the second and fourth Friday of every month. Ma and Da went to the city to do the big shop on those days, to buy things not available in the village shop.

'Her emotions peaked and dipped with the approach or departure of those days, in the same way as the tide rises and falls with the waxing and waning of the moon. A week out and she was bristling, unapproachable, dangerous. A misspoken word led to a punch or a kick. I stayed as far from her as I could, but Maria's chores trapped her in the house, so she suffered the most. A week after and her rage abated, but even then, her temper might erupt.

'The Fridays when she drank were bastard hard days. Da would go to his room, and Maria and I tiptoed around her. Sometimes she'd be quiet, drink herself into unconsciousness and we'd be fine. The following days, Saturday and Sunday ... Ma would be flat on her back, snoring into the dank, dark plaster or propped up on pillows reading a book — she never left the bed on those days.

'For forty-eight hours we'd be free of her. A weekend when Maria, Da and I were a family.'

'What would you do, on those days?' Cathryn asks.

And so I tell her what I remember.

*

'Saturday, a summer morning: the sun was glimmering over the sea, and I was standing at the skylight pulling on my old clothes, jeans and a tee-shirt that smell of damp and cow shit. Maria was dressing behind the curtain; there was a lightness to her movements, she stretched like a cat and then the curtain swooshed back and she was grinning at me.

"Last one out is a rotten egg!"

'I grinned back and, foregoing socks, crammed my feet into white canvas runners, stained green with grass and black from muck, but Maria was already running down the stairs, teasing me. This morning, we could be loud, we could call out and laugh.

'Da was in the back kitchen, whistling. He'd

111

already done the heavy work, boiled the mash for the pigs and left it to cool in the barn, milked the cow and strained the milk through a muslin cloth into two big jugs. He was burning the arse out of the iron skillet, and the aroma of frying bacon and the crackle of sausages made us speed out into the yard to do our chores.

'Maria raced me to the drinkers. She stood with the hose, the scum of green on the surface separating to reveal the clear cool water beneath. I scooped a frog out and regarded its solemn face before it blinked and hopped out into the grass.

'A suckler cow came to investigate, dipping her nose into the trough. Maria splashed its ear with the hose and it lifted its large head to bawl in protest. I laughed.

"What's so funny, dummy?" Maria put her finger over the end of the hose and flicked it towards me, the fine spray making a shimmering rainbow and I danced back out of range.

'There was a desperation to our joy; we gorged on it, knowing that, though it was only beginning, it was finite.

'Maria ran to feed the pigs and I dashed after her to release the ducks and hens. They scuttled out, all noise and flapping, like children released from school, feathers flying and cackling. Inside the feather-house it was dark, the cloying warm stink of poultry tainting the summer air.

'The only light inside came from nail holes in the corrugated roof. Dust motes swirled upward, and the hot air itched my scalp. I worked to extract eggs from nest boxes, collecting them in the pouch of my jumper. I heard Maria already running from the barn. I grabbed the last egg and dashed for the sun, hindered by my fragile cargo.

'If I was in front, I would give no quarter, but this morning Maria won. She almost always did, but she waited for me, and we walked together past the machine shed and feather-house and to the door where The Lady in the Glass was reflecting sunlight and blue.

'Da fried everything; there was a homogeneity to all the food he cooked. He served it from the skillet to three plates — bacon, sausages, eggs and potatoes, all brown-black and steaming and we fell on it as though we'd never eaten anything so good.

'We crammed breakfast between slices of bread, butter melting from the heat, dripping back onto our plates and streaking our chins.

"What do you want to do today?" Da asked. As if there were a million possibilities. And so it seemed.'

*

'Sunday, winter evening: there was a deadness to the sky. The Liffey was low and rumbling and the pavement echoed our footsteps as we walked, tired, towards the multi-storey carpark. There was frost in the air, it stung my nostrils. Maria's breath rose as thick as Da's cigarette smoke. I replayed a scenes from the movie, Bedknobs and Broomsticks, imagining how it would be to be under the care of Miss Eglantine Price. I envy Charlie, Carrie and Paul. I envied their Blitz.

'There was a desperation to Sunday evening. We

loaded into the Ford pickup. The windscreen fogged from our breath until we reached Gardiner Street, and Da switched on the heater.

'My eyes grew heavy. Da drove, and Maria sat on the passenger side. I was crammed between them on the half seat. The silence stretched.

*

'It took an hour to drive home and when we arrived the yard was glistening with frost. Ma was standing at the front door, smiling. The scent of roast chicken wafted over her shoulder.

"Did you have a good time?" she asked.

'I nodded. Maria made no answer, as Ma ran her fingers up and down her arms, warming herself.

'The weekend was over.'

*

We treasured those Saturday mornings and Sunday afternoons. We stowed them away, horded them, like arctic explorers stuffing their packs with sustenance to see them through the ice and snow.

Before the killing

'Ok, let's go back to the house,' prompts Cathryn.

I nod and am immediately back there, describing it all to her.

'My leg ached; it was a familiar tug, as if it was twisting from its socket. Sweat rose on my forehead.

'I had to sit. The table and chairs didn't look like they would support my weight, so I limped to the stuffed couch under the window. It was covered in grit and cobwebs, but looked solid. I collapsed into it raising dust, but all that mattered was the pain and the need to rest: a moment to catch my breath and then I could keep going. The journey was everything, a purging, an exorcism. And I only had that day.

Months in hospital had depleted my muscle tone; the lack of privacy, the monotony and the drugs had all drained me.

My dependency was my first struggle and it had almost broken me. I thought withdrawal was the worst pain I would ever face, but it wasn't. The resetting of bones, the surgery to fix and correct the damage I'd inflicted on myself was far worse. I wanted to die, to give up when the pain became unbearable.

I slept or dozed on the dusty couch. Maybe I dreamed; images may have flickered beneath my eyelids, or ghosts whispered in my ears. I heard Maria's laughter pitched like a wind chime on a light breeze; I saw her smile that broke my heart, and her imperfect beauty. I wanted to reach out and hug and kiss her, but even in my sleep I knew she wasn't real.

*

'We missed school often. Da needed us on the farm, or we wore scars or bruises that we had to hide. On the days we attended, we were seen as different. Beyond the house, and on the road that led to the village, school and harbour, we appeared dull and rough. Teachers claimed Maria was slow. But she wasn't; she just didn't care what they thought. A part of her accepted silence; she spun it, wrapped it around herself and me.

'We hid the broken parts of ourselves under rough edges, foul language and laughter. We met the world with bristling fists and acid tongues. Both of us became rocks, impregnable.

'Later Maria would learn to remove herself, to float clear of her surroundings. At school she became bovine in her attitude — kept her head bowed and eyes averted, speaking only on rare occasions. At home she took herself to that place we called Elsewhere.'

*

But before that, while we were still a family — broken, dysfunctional but still striving — we developed our own strategies to become invisible. We learned to become ethereal, and merge into the background. What had begun as an act of self-protection, over time became habitual. My addiction would claw its way to the surface later, but Maria's came earlier. She stayed Elsewhere, she became her own refuge. She retreated, hid herself from the pain. But that would all come later.

*

In the meantime, Maria was a warrior. When Ma hung washing on the line, we would crouch in the long grass, playing Indians or cowboys, Chicago mobsters or G-men. With imaginary bows or guns we would shoot her, riddle her full of lead and blow the smoke off our six-shooters.

Maria thwarted Ma and got away with it. She hid her whiskey, put mice in her bed, replaced the fresh milk with sour so it curdled the tea that Ma drank many times a day. We'd crouch in the garden's wilderness waiting for the shriek or the scream and we'd cling to each other, restraining our laughter, tears running down our cheeks at these small victories.

*

'You were in the front room. What happened next?' Cathryn interrupts my reverie.

'I think I fell asleep, or dozed. I woke disorientated, unsure where I was. It was darker, so I had slept for some time. There was a shape on the wall, a print, I'd forgotten it – long-horned cows, a herd, some in the foreground, large and distinct, others in the background, half drawn, heads down drinking from a silver blue lake, and behind them a range of mountains emerging from mist or fog.'

Those cows stood a silent witness to it all, to our lives; from their gilded frame they looked down on a family destroying itself. They were the only audience when, fuelled by whiskey and history, Ma gave in to bitterness and madness.

Beyond the front room, beyond the bright red bloodstone is the back kitchen and the scullery.

'When you woke, what did you do?'

'I sat up, my head spinning. There was a door leading to a hallway, short and dark. It was only four quick strides from one end to the other, but I hesitated. I'd never entered that hall of my own will. I only went there when Ma screamed out for me.'

Even as I speak, describing it to Cathryn, I feel a familiar tightness in my gut. The fear of being in a dangerous place and wanting to leave before I take the first step. My fists clench as I see myself enter, and my voice trembles.

'It was different, no longer inhabited by the living. I had time, I didn't need to rush. I assured myself that no harm could come, no evil seep from the walls. That was all in the past. Still, it was a dark place.

'Something feral scuttled overhead, I looked up into a tangle of webs, and moaned. I dropped the pretence and admitted to the power the place still had over me.'

Cathryn is leaning forward, her face unreadable. I look away as I continue.

'I made my way to Ma's room. Maria called it the dragon's lair, the centre of the web that Ma ensnared us in. My fear was that of a child, the contents of my stomach turned to bile. I tried not to see her, but she was there, her forehead damp and beaded with sweat from the fever. Ma had damaged herself in the most horrible, brutal fashion. She is sick, not from whiskey – but something worse. She has done something awful and now she is paying in sweat and blood and fever.'

Middlemarch

'Wait! You've skipped too far forward.' Cathryn looks flustered, but her voice is gentle.

I shrug and then remember a different morning.

'It was a Monday morning, mid-cycle, when Ma was usually tense and keyed up. But that morning she was quiet.'

'What do you remember?'

I picture the scene and fix it in my mind.

'She was sitting at the table, her toast buttered but untouched, holding a mug of tea held under her nose as though she's sniffing it, with her eyes half closed.'

'Was there anyone else there?'

I shake my head. 'No. Da was working with Uncle Paul that day.'

I imagined them out ahead of a running wave, the Mary J dipping and swooping like a bird.

'I sat down, Ma said nothing. She was too quiet and I was immediately eager to eat and go. Like a person who lived close to a volcano, I sensed the change, the deep-down rumblings.

' Something was different; a new depression had descended, like grey clouds gathering above the house. I bolted my toast and grabbed my bag. I turned back but Maria stayed in the back kitchen.'

'So Maria was there?'

I am uncertain for a moment, and then I nod.

'Yes. But not at the table.'

'Was she getting ready to go to school too?'

I recalled Maria's voice on the first day she stayed home.

'Time for you to grow up, pipsqueak,' she'd smiled. 'I done taught you all I could, now ye gotta fight your own battles!'

And she'd tipped the brim of her imaginary Stetson, smiling though her eyes were sad and distant.

'No,' I answer Cathryn. 'Maria hadn't been to school for weeks.'

'Ok, go ahead.'

'The road was lonely without her, and scarier, my shell easier to crack. I remember wishing I had been free too. I dragged my feet as I passed the feather-house, the machine shed and then the hen-house. But Maria was no freer than the chickens and ducks still locked inside — poultry that Ma strangled when they stopped laying and that we had with roast potatoes and honey glazed vegetables every second Sunday night.'

'You went to school alone?'

'Yes.'

'School was difficult for me, for both of us. The teachers and most of the older pupils knew, but none of them spoke about it or asked if we were ok. When I was alone, without Maria, I wasn't brave.'

I pause for breath.

*

'That day dragged. It was December, and the light was oppressive; there was no sun, only grey, and no sense of time passing, as if a perpetual twilight hung over the world. The classroom was full of the stench

120

of coal smoke and farting, sweating children — a fog that mirrored the grey of the clouds. Three o'clock wound in like a broken reel, and I remember thinking that the clock resented each tick, rising from the six to the twelve, then falling back towards the half hour.

'When I got home, I saw the pickup in the yard, so I knew Da was back. I jumped the side wall and came through the orchard. I unlatched the door, smelling the salt. In the back kitchen, eight mackerel were floating in the sink, spines poking through the blood pink nimbus of water. I dumped my bag behind the door.

'Ma was still sitting in the front room. Da was sitting beside her and I could see by the set of his face that he'd sensed the change too.'

I draw a long breath and compose myself.

'He — Da — was more aware of her than we were. We only watched for the dragon but he paid attention to Ma. He loved … '

I hesitate, a lump forming in my throat. He loved her; how else could he tolerate her, allow her to do the things she did?

Cathryn makes a note while I continue.

'He was looking at her in a way he seldom did, smiling in that sardonic, melancholic way of his. Ma's face is cold, expressionless. I retreat, slip out to the back and jump the wall. I ran to my chores without changing into my working clothes.'

'Were you punished for that?'

'Yes.' I don't want to talk about it and Cathryn doesn't insist.

*

121

I remember her words, 'You're a fucking disgrace, do you hear me?' and her hand stinging as it connected with my cheek.

'Do you think I have nothing to do but wash?' she'd continued.

There was pain, a momentary suspension, when stars and darkness fought for attention.

'That'll teach you to change into your working clothes.' Her chest had heaved as though the effort had exhausted her.

She'd not eaten her mackerel, and Da had lifted it from the table and scraped it into the bowl for Gráinneog.

Later, after she had gone to bed, I had sat on the couch with Da. I stayed close, taking strength from him, though he said nothing about what had happened.

*

'Maria knew, she understood,' I say to Cathryn. 'I don't know how, but she did.

'That night I lay in bed, my cheek red and my spine stinging from the grooves Ma's nails had carved along my vertebrae. In the bed opposite, Maria twisted and turned..

"Are you ok?" she asked.

'I nodded into the darkness and then realised that she couldn't see me.

'I wasn't all right; I was trembling. Something was up with Ma. I couldn't define it, but I said "Yes," because we denied pain, we didn't let it in.

"She's pregnant," Maria whispered, sobbing.

"How do you know?" I asked.

Maria didn't answer.

"God," I said to the near darkness.

'I was almost fourteen; I knew where babies came from. I'd grown up around livestock; I understood the mechanics. But as I lay shivering, listening to Maria sob, I could not imagine Ma giving birth, or caring for a baby.

'We were flesh and bone proof that she had been a mother, that she had gone through labour. But I had no memory of it t and could not imagine it.

'I didn't remember her nursing me, changing me or bathing me. I have no memory of maternal love. Did those things ever happen? I remember hardness, a scathing tongue.

'I ran my fingers over the heat of my cheek, and I search for memories of something else. All that came was an image of Da lifting me from the bed — his strong arms hugging me close, his whispering in my ear, hushing me.

'Or Maria bathing and dressing me when I was too small to do those things for myself.

'How young was she when she tended me? Had she ever been a child herself? I slunk from my bed and climbed in beside Maria. She was still awake, and I half expected her to eject me from the narrow bed, but instead she reached out and pulled me closer, clinging. Her pillow was wet with tears. Her heart was beating against my ribs, and then it slowed, matching mine and her hold relaxed, and we slept.'

*

'So,' prompts Cathryn, 'when you entered the hallway, you were reminded of that?'

'No,' I answer. I imagine myself back there now. 'Or, maybe, in part.'

'Go on, tell me.'

'The room was dark. The single, small, recessed window so fouled with grime and webs that the light that entered it was almost mustard, a grey, yellow acid light that tinged the room sepia. Plasterboard hung from above. Something that lived in the ceiling registered my presence; there was a skittering sound, and a shower of dust and grit onto the already littered floor. I tried not to think about what I had disturbed. The wall to the right was bare, damp as sweat. A chill as subtle as that of an open fridge seeped from it.

*

'The floor was bare concrete. I remembered a carpet there; I looked for and then saw it, rolled up and moved against the back wall; dark and decaying, it merged into the drab wall. Again, I wondered who placed it there. There was a a book on top, its edges curled, the pages plump with dampness. I took a step closer and picked it up: Middlemarch.

'I remembered Maria reading out loud, late at night, and us huddling beneath a pile of blankets. I heard her voice:

> 'In Mr. Brooke the hereditary strain of
> Puritan energy was clearly in abeyance;
> but in his niece Dorothea it glowed
> alike through faults and virtues, turning
> sometimes into impatience of her
> uncle's talk or his way of "letting things
> be" on his estate.'

I hesitate for a minute. The memory triggers another — Ma leaving a book on the kitchen table, and her voice: 'I'm finished this, you can throw it in the bin.'

She knew Maria would take it, but she wouldn't make a gift of it, wouldn't concede even that much.

My jaw clamps; I'm still angry at her spite.

'Ma gave us very little,' I explain. 'But she was a reader, and we became readers. I recall nights when we escaped into the words of Dorothea, or Pip or David Copperfield. Maria reading, and me lying on my back, imagining myself a reformer, a circus performer or a castaway on a desert island.

'I replaced the book on the remnant of carpet and moved back to the door. Wallpaper clung to the right-hand wall, pink cabbage roses on a background that was once beige but was now lurid orange. Where wall met ceiling, two sheets were peeling back, hanging down over themselves, as though bowing to the bed.

'I stood on the threshold, not wanting to enter. I could see everything from where I was. The door was flush against the back wall, and anything lurking behind it would have eight legs or twitching whiskers.

'The mattress was askew on the bed, and the metal base was red with rust, springs visible. It was bare but for a single pillow, striped black and grey. The inner edge of the bed has collapsed … '

Perversely, I remembered a girl I once loved: Abbey. I heard her giggling when a different bed collapsed beneath us. Her arm was about my neck as we tilted inward, her legs slipping over mine as we glided to the floor. She was laughing, her face screwed up in a smile, her eyes dazzling in the sunlight.

*

My face must have dropped. I had been loath to think of Abbey in that place that contained only bile.

Da's room

I've no memory of my parents sleeping together, but Maria and I were proof that they had. I shudder, imagining a liaison fuelled by desire and alcohol, their coming together a rushed and brutal clash. I imagine my father escaping from her clutches afterwards, scuttling back, soiled and dirty, to his own refuge at the end of the dark silent hall. The snapping jaws of the mantis pursuing him.

But he didn't see her that way. He loved her; yes, he loved her.

I blink. A tear of anger rolls down my cheek and I swipe it away. I'm angry that Da treated her well, opened doors for her, held her coat for her; and angry that his attention only ever earned a snide rebuff. Ma was incapable of graciousness. But he loved her, no matter how much I wished otherwise.

Cathryn clears her throat. 'Do you need a break?' I shake my head, afraid if I stop I will not continue.

*

'Da's room was at the end of the hall. I could hear him call, "Are you all right? Maria?"

'Christ! Pathetic empty words from a pathetic empty man but then, how could I judge him without judging myself? I was young, yes, but I was strong. I should have done something, tried at least, but I didn't.'

I close my eyes, taking a deep breath.

'That's what I struggled with later. It became the cornerstone of my addiction, the excuse and the justification. I'd let my sister take the beating, let her suffer. And I'd been too afraid to help ... '

'That's not helpful, Dan. Tell me about your father's room.'

And so I continue.

'Da never lifted a hand against either Maria or myself. But he would slink away when Ma was at her most dangerous, leaving us to fend for ourselves. When she lashed out and hurt us, he was not there to save us. Da knew; he saw the blood, the bruises. He wasn't vicious like Ma, but nor did he intervene; he didn't save us. But, fuck it all, he was the closest thing to a loving parent we had, he was the only softness in an otherwise hard, miserable house.'

I pause for breath, realising my voice has risen. Cathryn says nothing.

'That was his saving grace,' I continue. 'The love he showed was real, but it didn't make him strong. He was a weak man, and never fought back against the ugliness in our lives.

'I remember softness, though; I remember love — him sitting with me when I lay in bed, my body aching.

'Maria suffered more, but I didn't escape. And whatever had caused it, it had been bad; I remember that much. Ma had been at her worst, her temper ignited by a mix of anger and the gnawing need for whiskey — those flailing, beating hands. She'd hurt me, sliced a deep grove into the flesh of my arm.

It healed, and the bruises faded. But the memories don't fade, the hurt never heals.'

My voice shakes, and I pause, drawing a deep breath.

'Da sat beside me that night, his eyes full of misery and sympathy. But he never acknowledged how our lives were; he never accepted that we were being destroyed, or the things Ma did to us.

"Don't hate her Danny," he'd say. I despised him for that. It was only at the end that he admitted all that had happened but by then it was far too late.'

'So you went to his room,' Cathryn prompted. 'What did you find?'

'Da's room was better preserved; it seemed as if he'd just left. He was a neat man, tidy in his habits and it showed in the space he'd occupied. His suits still hung in the wardrobe, dusty, moth eaten, but everything was still neat. Two pairs of dusty shoes poked out from under the single bed. Da was fastidious, and cared about his appearance; he wore old clothes while working but even those clothes he kept neat.'

Again I pause for breath, I am thinking about a father who did his best, was as much a victim as we were.

'Did you blame him for what happened?'

'Bingo, the sixty-four-million-dollar question!' I shrug. 'Yes, I blamed him, but I could never hate him, though I tried.'

I try to explain; I want to be fair to him and want Cathryn to understand that Da was different afterwards.

'Yes, I blamed him for what happened. He knew, so he was complicit in it all. But still … when you only have one parent who shows you love, that's who you cling to.

'Later, after Maria and Ma disappeared, he changed. He did his best to protect me, did everything he could to keep me safe. He was softer, more tactile; sometimes I saw him looking at me and I could see the love in his face, his eyes soft, his smile, not sardonic as it used to be but... almost shy. Come to think of it, I'm not sure he'd known much affection himself — my memory of Agnes is of a hard, mean-mouthed bitch.'

Cathryn nods and takes more notes.

'Anything else?'

'No. I left his room and walked back along the hall, the four strides that span an ocean of loathing, fear and gnawing regret. And the knowledge that somewhere amid it all I had lost Maria. She disappeared in slow increments — slipped away to Elsewhere. Even before she disappeared, she became The Lost.

'I was back in the front room, railing against a broken childhood that no words could fix, and against things broken that will remain forever broken. No glue, no kisses and hugs can fix that damage.'

'Don't you think that's dramatic?'

'Do you?' I spit back.

She considers. 'Maybe not. What happened next?'

'I went back into the front room. I collapsed again onto the musty coach and I surrendered to emotion.'

She arches an eyebrow.

'I cried!' I answer. 'I cried for all of us, for my lost sister, my father and myself. But I didn't cry for her, the bitch who brought us all so low. No, fuck her! I would have hacked her to pieces if I could have. I had not one iota of love for her. Even now, all I have is a hate and loathing, and I'm not ashamed of it.'

*

I pause. 'Except ... I believe I'm a good person, a spiritual one, yet I have space in my heart for a hatred so complete and so extreme that it frightens me.'

A Saturday in Dublin

Cathryn looks at the clock. It is 10.45 am.

'I need a coffee. Do you fancy one?'

I nod.

'Let's go to the coffee shop across the street.'

'I know it,' I answer. 'The waitress there pities me; she thinks I'm a cripple.' Cathryn smiles at that and the room grows brighter; I look into her eyes and the gloom lifts completely.

*

The waitress recognises me. She eyes Cathryn, her glance wandering over her faded jeans and over-large shirt, and widen as she reassesses. I'm unsure if I've risen or plummeted in her estimation of me. I smile.

'Grab a seat there, love,' she says.

We move to the back of the café. There's only one other customer — an old man who sits reading his newspaper, his coffee cup empty, crumbs of pastry trickling down his cardigan towards his liver-spotted hands. He pays us no notice.

At the back of the café, windows open out onto the street. The cloud is high and silver grey, the sun a faint haze. The city has a Saturday quietness about it, there is no sense of urgency as pedestrians amble by.

Cathryn takes the inside seat, near the red leatherette that lines the entire back wall. I sit opposite her. She shakes her hair out, combing her fingers through it quickly and efficiently, capable of plaiting unseen strands almost unconsciously, aware of herself in that way that all women seem to be.

The waitress appears at my side.

'What can I get ye?'

I order coffee but Cathryn surprises me by ordering a full breakfast.

'I didn't have time earlier.' She smiles when I look at her. 'Jen is so tetchy in the morning, she hates delays. It isn't worth making something and eating it in the car. I usually drop her, go into town, grab breakfast and wander around the shops until it's time to pick her up.'

I nod. I've no frame of reference for this; small talk is beyond me, but I enjoy listening to her.

'On Sunday she helps me at home, laundry, dusting, vacuuming.'

I'm a little surprised, and perhaps it shows..

She shrugs, chin on her fist. 'We enjoy doing it. I grew up in a large family — there were eight of us we all chucked in, otherwise it would have been chaos. My mum died when I was fifteen. I was the eldest and my father, bless him, he worked all day and then came home to more work, cooking and organising eight kids.'

She stalled. 'I'm sorry, Dan. I shouldn't be talking about this.'

'Why? Your Dad sounds great. It can't have been easy for him.'

She considers me for a moment. Something shifts, like the moment between the tick-tock, the pause, then the advance.

'Yes.' She smiles. 'He was. Dad was an incredible man, he encouraged us all, wanted us to be the best we could be. When I came over here to study, he encouraged me, even though it left him with more to do. My youngest sister was only eleven, and the rest of them lived at home. Two of the lads still do.'

'He must be proud of you?'

Her smile fades.

'Yes, he is, I suppose. He's proud of what I've made of myself, professionally. He was the one who encouraged me to consider private practice.'

'Jen was a baby — I think he envisaged me working from home.' She tells me how she had worked in the hospital before leaving to set up on her own, but I haven't forgotten her earlier hesitancy.

'My family life, my marriage, Jen. It hasn't all been straightforward; Dad has struggled to understand it all, and disagrees with some of my decisions.'

Again, I can only nod. I'm in a foreign country, and the language is strange.

'Don't pretend you don't know!' She smiles, but her eyes are sad. 'You're a clever guy, Dan, you read the papers — every bastard and his dog knows my marriage is a disaster, that my husband is screwing another woman.'

'I'm sorry.' I'm lost, I want to say something comforting, something solid.

'He's a fool,' is the best I can manage.

But she smiles, her eyes bright again.

'Thank you.'

The moment passes. The waitress arrives with

the coffee and Cathryn's breakfast and I watch in fascination as she attacks her food with gusto.

'Sorry!' she exclaims. 'I'm starving.'

*

'So, you were telling me, your mother was pregnant?'

'Maria believed she was, and Da was being ... careful of her.'

We'd left the café. Cathryn was meeting her daughter on O'Connell Street. 'Are you ok to walk that far, or should I hail a cab?'

'I'm fine,' I say, buttoning my coat. The wind had changed direction and the clouds were thickening out to the east.

'Good,' she says, but steadies my arm. 'So, tell me about it.'

*

I imagine the morning: the cold crispness, and Ma standing in the front room, lips pursed and eyes cold as diamonds.

'Ma's eyes were blazing; she was angry, her jaw set like the prow of a juggernaut on an unalterable course.

"I'm taking her to the doctor," Da told us before they left. He looked sad, or maybe resigned. He followed her out of the house, his shoulders stooped and head hanging. We stood at the skylight and looked down on them. Da opened the car door for her, acting the part of the gentleman, as always; he tried hard, but like us, he fell short.

'As they got into the car, I pressed my face to the window. I kept my eye on Da, waiting for them to leave. He said something, and her reaction was anger. I wondered why; she was having a baby, but she showed no softness or pleasure, only a grim-faced determination. When I looked at Maria, she was pale and anxious, eyes riveted on some point visible only to her. As though in a trance, she was chanting the same words over and over :

"She'll hurt it, she'll hurt it."

'Tears streamed down her face and her thin body was trembling.

'As the car disappeared, I looked after it and knew that Ma intended to do something awful. Maria's hands were on my shoulders, squeezing. Darkness closed about us.

'Ma had left us no chores, but the hours of freedom ahead seemed like a penance, not a gift.'

The killing

'Da ran away, left us when we needed him the most. I didn't see him, only heard the car door slamming as he dropped her off and the sound of the engine as he left. Ma walked across the yard, head up, stepping out like a soldier marching towards the enemy, blood already in her eye. When she came into the house, she carried two bags, and the sound of bottles clinking was like a death knell.

'I hunkered down in the darkness at the bannister rail, Ma muttered to herself as she unpacked the bags. I was used to the gold labels and tops of whiskey bottles, but this was different — the labels were yellow and the spirit was not the amber hue I recognised, but clear. Ma slammed the two bottles on the table.

'She stalked to the kitchen, swearing and shouting. Then she reappeared, dragging the big tin bath to the front room and set it by the table. She opened the first bottle, shouting for Maria to come. Maria was behind me on the bannister, eyes shut tight and head shaking.

"Where are you, you fucking bitch?" screamed Ma.

'I tried to grab Maria, but she ran down the stairs. I listened to Ma's harsh voice, telling her to light the fire and turn on the boiler.

'She sat at the table, opened the first bottle, and

wrinkling her nose, drank straight from the neck. She took something from a pill case and washed it down with more of the spirit — it was gin, but I didn't know that then; it looked like water.

'I stayed where I was. I understood that something terrible was happening, but I didn't know what.'

Cathryn's arm tightens on mine as I continue.

'I retreated further up the steps. I felt the tension; it sparked and crackled, like static, as though something dark and evil had come into the house. I looked away, fearful of drawing her attention. Afraid, not of her, but of what she would do. She drank more. She did it without pleasure, her movements mechanical, lifting the bottle and swallowing, her throat working, gagging against it, her hand wiping her mouth, her eyes bright as burning coals.

'Maria lit the fire, the boiler hissed, and she ran up the stairs and sat beside me. Her body trembled and something else, I remember — her fists, she was clenching and unclenching them, her face twisting. She was trying to stifle sobs and, when they came, they were awful, like the death throes of an animal.

'She knew, but I didn't, not yet. I didn't appreciate the potential of an unborn life, or what was to come. It was not until much later that I understood what had happened that night. In retrospect, I can see the shadow of the days to come, creeping from the dark corners of the front room where my mother sat drinking gin.'

*

'Ma screamed for Maria again. She was drunk, roaring.

"Where the fuck are you?" she screamed. "Come, fill the bath for me. And hot, as hot as you can make it!"

'Maria froze beside me, sobbing. But Ma kept screaming.

'I didn't want her to go; I clung to her, but she pushed my hands away. She wouldn't look at me, but turned and ran down the stairs, shoulders heaving, silently.

'Ma didn't notice or didn't care. Maria carried buckets of water, filling the bath until it was full. Ma leaned from her chair testing the temperature of the water with her hand.

"No. It's not hot enough!" she screamed. "I want it scalding! Do you understand? Hot enough to strip skin!" She tipped the water out onto the flags, steam rose and she lashed out at Maria. The sound of the slap was like the snap of a leather belt and Maria stumbled, an angry red welt rising on her cheek.

"I want it scalding hot, do you hear me?"

'Maria looked numb. Blood streamed from her nose, and tears streaked her cheeks, but she did what Ma asked. She drew water from the boiler, buckets of it, scalding hot and steamy. The fire was roaring, and the front room roiling with heat and humidity.

'Ma tested the water again. She jerked her hand back from it, then rounded on Maria.

"'Get out!" she spat, and Maria recoiled, holding her hands before her, her face contorted with fear.

"Get out and stay out, no matter what you hear."

'Ma glanced up to where I sat in darkness. "Or what you see!" she screamed. "Don't come back into this room!"

'She glared at Maria. "Do you understand?"

' Maria nodded.

"Say it!" Ma screamed again. "Fucking say it, idiot! Do you understand?"

"Yes!" Maria screamed back at her, then ran up the stairs and sat beside me, hugging me tightly.

'We stayed there, on the top of the stairs, clinging to each other, scared but unable to turn away.

'Oh, my sweet Jesus!' Cathryn grabbed my arm, her eyes wide. 'She knew you were there?'

I nod, too deep into the story to stop.

'Yes, she knew, the fucking cunt knew we were there. She swore as she lowered her hard, white, naked body down into the steaming bath, redness flushing her skin, flaring across her thighs, belly and breasts.

"Die, you bastard!" she cried.

'The second bottle of gin was on the chair by the bath. "Die!" She kept roaring as she drank, the gin feeding her fury. "Die!" She drained the bottle, dropped it on the floor, and it rolled across the flags, banging against the grate. Then she took a pin — like a shirt pin but larger — and she did something to herself, reaching down between her legs, and the bathwater turned pink.

'I wanted to turn away, but I felt paralysed.

'She lifted herself from the bath. Maria stood, and when she reached out and touched my arm I flinched, and she pulled away.

'Ma was bleeding, her legs splattered, the pinkness of it running in rivulets, on her feet, on the wet flags.

'She didn't dry herself; she stumbled and almost fell; she grabbed out, pulled herself onto the couch. Her skin was raw, her stomach red and angry.'

*

I pause, shutting my eyes. The world spins around me and I focus on the weight of Cathryn's hand on my arm; it pulls me back, but I shake my head, I have to finish it.

*

'She hit herself. She joined her balled fists, hitting, and every time she did, she grunted, the sound of breath forced from her body.

'"Die!" she screamed, punctuating the blows with screams. "Die! Die!"

*

'Ma killed the baby, she took its life and with it, the last of her own humanity. And the damage reached out, wrapped itself about Maria. I saw her beside me, trembling, her mouth slack. She dragged me backward.

"Come," she begged. "Please."

'She dragged me from the bannister rails.

"You need to forget this," she whispered. "Put it away somewhere safe, where it can't hurt you."

'She spoke as if I might bundle the madness up and toss it in a drawer, forgotten.

'I watched the light fade from her eyes; she was Elsewhere — a deeper Elsewhere, and her eyes were blank, as though a curtain had fallen inside her.'

Dead and gone

We're standing, the city coalescing around us. I look at Cathryn. She's squeezing my hand, and tears are streaming down her face.

'Oh, Jesus Christ, Dan.' I know now that Maria had never told her.

A girl walks up to us.. 'Hey, mum.'

Cathryn pulls her hand away from mine and turns to face her daughter, a teenage version of her mother. Cathryn wipes her eyes with the sleeve of her jacket, blaming the wind. I look at the girl, smiling coyly. The scene is so ordinary. Another girl is standing off, watching us — her friend, I realise.

'Amanda is going to the film, she's with some of her friends, would you mind if I go with them?'

Cathryn's face drops.

'You don't have to wait, we can get the train home.'

Cathryn opens her mouth, but her daughter beats her to it.

'There'll be a gang of us, so I'll be safe.' She smiles. 'Please, mum.'

Cathryn smiles back. 'Go to the movie, but I'll pick you up when it's over.'

Jen, or Jennifer, scowls, then shrugs, and finally kisses Cathryn before turning towards me.

'Bye,' she says, acknowledging me with a flick of

her hand.

Cathryn stares at me. I'm aware of the potential for damage, a wrong word or look.

'She stood me up.' She shakes her head. 'My own daughter!'

'It happens,' I say. 'Let's go for a drink.' She stares at me, raising her eyebrows.

'Not for me.' I wink. 'For you. I think you need one!'

She laughs, and I know I've saved her from this small hurt.

*

We settle down in the corner. The lounge is dim after the bright light outside. Apart from an elderly couple at a table some way from us, the place is empty. There are muffled roars and groans from the bar, with the tinny voice of a TV commentator. I'm not a soccer fan; I understand a little about the game but, like my father, I'd been a rugby enthusiast, following the provincial and the national team. But I have fallen out of touch with it now.

I lost so much to alcohol. And now, I'm in a bar for the first time since leaving the hospital. The distinctive aroma of stale beer lingers in the air, beneath it the sweeter aroma of whiskey. I take a sip from my Coke and smile at Cathryn.

'Are you sure you're ok?' There's genuine concern in her voice. She orders a red wine and then changes her mind, asking for a soda water and saying something to the barman about a woman's prerogative.

When we're settled, she looks at me, worried;

my story's left a mark. There's another click, the pendulum stills again, and something shifts.

'How did you cope? What happened next?' Cathryn's eyes glint.

I think about the morning after — Ma pale as death, Da downcast, and Maria standing on the bloodstone, expressionless, her eyes vacant.

"It's gone." That's all Ma said. The kitchen was so quiet, as though we feared to make a sound. I remember the clock ticking, a log in the stove collapsing sideways and sending sparks up the chimney. There was a surreal calmness.'

I turn towards Cathryn.

'We'd … Maria and I, had experienced the worst of human nature. But still we were not beyond shock or surprise; some things could still shake our world and leave us breathless.

"Dead and gone,' Ma repeated. Her voice was startling, abrupt and firm; there was a finality to it. She sipped her tea, her eyes dark-rimmed and bloodshot, dark circles under her eyes. I wished her dead for what she'd done, not just to us, but to Da too. He'd left us, but I couldn't hate him for it. He knew what she would do and that he couldn't stop it, so he ran away.

Da crept back long afterwards, when Maria and I lay huddled beneath a blanket, her hand gripping mine so hard it hurt, but I couldn't pull it away, and didn't want to.

He was mumbling swear words, his breath quick and anxious. He emptied the bloody water from the tub, and I remember it sluicing down the kitchen sink. And then I heard him sob. I never told him I'd heard him; I wish now I had, but I didn't know how. There was a grunt as he lifted her and carried her to her bed.

'He'd done what he had to, he'd cleaned the kitchen, mopped the water from the front room. He looked like he hadn't slept and then sat at the table, head down. When Ma spoke, he never looked up or acknowledged her words. I think he wanted her to be quiet; if she was, he could deny what had happened. He flinched as she spoke as though she'd spat at him. I saw his face harden, and he stood up. I thought he might hit her, and wished that he would, but he turned away, not looking at any of us, and walked towards the door.

'But she didn't let him leave. Her fists clenched as she banged them on the table, the cups and plates rattling. 'You knew what I'd do!' she roared bitterly. 'I did it before, and I'd do it again.'

'Maria still stood on the bloodstone, her fist clenching and unclenching. Her face was bone white, her eyes squeezed shut.

"What did you want?" Ma asked.

'Da stopped at the door, his back to her.

"Look what happens when they live!" Ma's laugh was spiteful.

'Da spun around, his face bloodless.

"No, Caroline." He begged her not to go on, but she did.

"Did you want another imbecile like this one?" She jutted her chin out at Maria.

"Or another useless bastard like the lad here?"

145

She banged her open palm on the table.

'Da collapsed against the door frame. A moan, long and drawn out, escaped from him. He shook his head, looking at me and at Maria, denying what she'd said. But it was too late.

'After a few minutes, Ma stood and cleared the table, then brushed past Maria. And just like that it was over. Ma was no longer pregnant, the subject was closed, and we would never speak of it again.'

'Jesus, she'd done it before.' Cathryn looks numb.

I nod, and tell her about the aftermath.

*

'It wasn't over, not for Maria. The night Ma killed the baby damaged her, changed her. No, it started before that, on the day she discovered Ma was pregnant. Maria knew, maybe not everything, but enough. She knew what would happen; Ma had made her complicit in it.

'Little by little Maria hardened, like some warped pearl, building up layer upon layer that leached away all the goodness and bravery, the art, the joy, the laughter and mischief, all the things I loved about her. It was all locked away in her own Elsewhere. What she left behind was a shadow of my beautiful sister; she was still fearless, but joyless too. She didn't speak, didn't look at anyone, didn't respond to anything. She was numb.

'Ma never wanted children, never wanted us, hated us for surviving. That pushed Maria to the edge.'

Cathryn takes a sip of her drink; I can see she is horrified.

'The house stayed quiet for a long time; the death hung over it, like a shroud. Ma was sick, she'd damaged herself — fever and infection took hold of her, wracked her body and later her mind. She raved, and gripped by a madness of a different sort, she suffered, bled and sweated. And when I saw her hard, thin body contort, I took pleasure in her agony, I wanted her to die. But she didn't. At night she screamed, waking to whatever fever-driven nightmares fed her insanity. She cried out for her father and mother, she called out to others, names of people none of us knew.

'She fouled herself with shit and piss and blood; the house reeked of death and corruption, but she refused to let Da call a doctor.

'Maria cared for her, bathed her and cleaned her, she fed her and mopped her brow. Maria nursed the bitch who had tried to kill her before she drew a breath. She ministered to her, took care of her sick, rotten body. Ma was ill, but Maria was broken, the bleakness of her expression, the blankness of her eyes. She was slipping away from me and I couldn't reach her.'

*

'Maria didn't speak to anyone for weeks. She walked from room to room, unresponsive, as though she didn't see her surroundings. She ate almost nothing — she'd always been thin but when she stripped at night, she was skeletal; her shoulders and hips were round nubs of bone, her ribs prominent. It frightened Ma; she'd never broken Maria, but this

147

was different — Maria no longer feared her at all, or reacted to her; she'd passed beyond hurt. She tried to goad Maria into responding to her, and even though Da and I could see what Maria had become, Ma wouldn't have it.

'She hammered Maria, she punched her and pummelled her; she scratched and tore and bit — it was sickening, the brutality. But Maria stood mute to it all, unfeeling, accepting it and shrugging it off. Her face was devoid of expression, scabs built one on another, old bruises disappeared under fresh ones, livid purple and black.

'I tried to protect her, and it was only then that she showed any reaction, pulling me back, away from Ma. She was thin but still strong. And Ma tested her, raved at her, mocked her, but still it made no difference.

'And then, Ma stopped.'

*

'The change came like a shifting wind, and I saw it. Ma was frightened of Maria, she feared her own daughter's contempt and indifference. It wasn't mercy that stayed her hands, her feet and her tongue, but a kind of wonderful terror.'

Cathryn looks at her watch and swears. 'Jesus, I've forgotten Jen.'

This time I tease her, and she laughs. It sounds good; it lightens a day darkened by clouds from above and within.

I walk with her to the door. Outside, we are greeted by brightness; the sky is blue with swathes of cumulus sailing across it. The cinema is just across the road and Cathryn spots her daughter and waves. Jen is still with her friends.

'When do you want me to come in again?' I ask, before she goes to cross the street.

'I'll phone you.' She finds a break in the traffic and darts across. I watch her reach the girl, her voice faint. She reaches out and puts an arm about her daughter. They're laughing at something and then Jennifer links arms with her mother's and they walk away, and I feel a crushing sense of loneliness.

I look back at the pub, consider it for a moment, then shake my head: it would be too easy. I turn towards home.

Falling in love

It's Monday morning and I am back in Cathryn's office.

'We're friends now, Cathryn. Right?'

She looks at me, one eyebrow raised.

'What's all this about?'

'Just answer the question,' I scowl. 'Are we friends or not?'

'We have a professional relationship, not a doctor–patient one, based as it is on the needs of a third party — '

'Yes,' I cut in. 'It's a professional relationship, but is it a friendly one?'

'It's not adversarial, if that's what you mean. Look, just tell me what's on your mind.'

I sigh. 'Can't you just give me a straight answer? I want to know if our … relationship is friendly.'

She smiles. 'And I've told you, Dan, it's professional; it's not adversarial, hence, I would say, so far it has been friendly.'

'Good, at long last.' I look at her, wondering how much I can get away with.

'I've been sitting here answering your questions for weeks now.'

She tries to speak, but I hold my hand up.

'I have a few questions I'd like answered. Only I'm not sure if we're friends, and a non-adversarial relationship, well … '

She stares at me, her eyes widening.

'If you have questions, ask them, there's no need for groundwork.'

I nod. 'Ok, tell me something about Maria.'

She considers. 'Like what?'

'Like anything. Give me something that lets me visualise her.'

'She's a teacher. She works in a school for kids with issues; she's also an artist, and paints the most wonderful but very dark scenes.'

'Anything else?'

Cathryn picks up my folder and looks at me, her eyes bright and intelligent.

'I'll tell you what. You tell me the rest of the history of Abigail Taylor and I'll answer two questions for you. You can ask me about Maria, but nothing personal.'

'But everything else is fair game?'

'Everything that doesn't reveal where she is, or who she is with. I will answer questions that don't compromise her. Agreed?'

I smile. 'Agreed.'

*

'Something happened in Paris.' Cathryn looks at her notes. 'You called it a blip. Tell me about it.'

I recall the day.

'It was late September. The sky over Paris was growing dark when we walked up the steps of the Sacré-Cœur. We'd been in the city for two weeks and would leave the next day. Russ was fed up, complaining about everything.

"If I see one more gallery or museum, I swear I'll

chuck."

"Well, why don't you fuck off so!" Abbey was becoming more pissed off at him, and it was clear he wasn't happy having me along.

"Sorry?" He was facing her; I didn't want them to fight, and felt it was my fault.

"Come on, let's go and see this church," I said. I was doing my best not to dislike Russ, but he wasn't making it easy.

*

'It was almost dark when we entered the Sacré-Cœur and inside we split up. I wanted to see the Apse Mosaic.'

I hesitate, trying to put the memory in order.

'Have you seen it?'

Cathryn shook her head. 'No, churches are not my thing.'

'Nor mine, but the Sacré-Cœur is amazing. I must have stood there for twenty minutes, lost in it. When I turned back towards the exit, I could see Russ lounging in a pew. He was glaring at Abbey who was lighting a candle beneath a statue of the Virgin, the light from a side window spilling in — that intense light of a setting sun — and she stood in a golden pool. Her expression was so perfect that I couldn't catch my breath.

'I knew then that I was falling in love with her, and the thought frightened me. I'd no experience of it, no idea how to express what I felt. When she saw me, she turned and smiled, her eyes shining. I think she knew. She walked towards me and took my hand and we went back to where Russ was waiting. When he saw us holding hands he looked up; I saw the pain in his eyes, and I knew then that he was in love with her too.

'When I told Abbey, she told me I was wrong. And later that night when we went on the Bateaux Mouche and all laughed so much, I convinced myself that it hadn't happened.

'The following morning Abbey wanted to go to the Rodin Museum. Russ moaned about going but didn't want to stay at the Pension alone, so Abbey suggested I hung out with him. I'd had my full of galleries too, so an easy morning was fine with me. That afternoon we were to catch the TGV to Milan. I'd already packed my gear and planned to chill out for the morning.

'Not long after Abbey left, Russ rolled a cigarette and took a deep drag. I suppose it was my own curiosity; I knew about weed but had never tried it.

"Take a hit," Russ offered. I did, and we finished it between us. I was light-headed, but I liked the feeling. Not long after he rolled another, but it was stronger, or I was unused to it.

'When Abbey came back, I'd passed out on the floor. When I came to, I heard Abbey s shouting at Russ, blaming him. 'He's not used to it!'

"Bullshit, he smoked the entire joint!"

'I stood up, but had to sit down on the edge of the bed. My head was spinning, and it unsettled my stomach.

"He's right.' I said. 'It's my fault. I didn't eat this morning, and I smoked too much of it.' Abbey was glaring at me; she didn't believe me.

"I told you," Russ scowled.

'Abbey was angry. She told us to sort ourselves out. We were late and only had an hour to get to Gare de Lyon. The tension between us was palpable.

'That night, as we travelled towards Milan, I drank for the first time in over a month. The weed messed me up; it didn't take much for me to get drunk. When Abbey saw me, the look on her face was awful. I could hear Russ talking to her, telling her that I was fine, that it would be ok.

'She went back to her seat and Russ disappeared. I stayed at the bar. I was angry with myself. I'd stopped drinking, but it was too late, I was already drunk — very drunk. The train was moving fast, and I didn't know which way our seats were. I wandered to the wrong end of the train, found an empty seat and fell asleep.

'When I woke some hours later it was close to daylight. Abbey was standing over me, shaking my shoulder.

"We're almost there. Are you ok?"

'The way she looked at me squeezed something in my chest. Her eyes were full of doubt and I wanted to tell her it would never happen again, to get up and hug her, but I didn't. Instead, I looked up at her. Then she hunkered down in the passage and hugged me. I can't even remember what she said. I remember clinging to her, inhaling her scent and swearing to myself that I would do nothing to hurt her.'

The wrong questions

'Did you tell Abbey how you felt?' Cathryn asks.

I draw a deep breath before answering. 'I did, but not straightaway.'

'When?'

'After Milan, when Russ left, and it was just the two of us.'

'So Russ left in Milan.'

I nod. 'When we got off the train, Abbey was walking between us. She turned to Russ and told him if he ever pulled anything like that again that he could fuck off. He said he was sorry, and I'm sure he meant it. We all stopped for a moment, the crowd from the train pouring around us and we hugged on the platform, all three of us. After that I thought things would be fine, but later that day, at Santa Maria delle Grazie, Russ made his announcement. We were standing in front of da Vinci's Last Supper, and he was pensive.

"I'm going to Hamburg," he said, as if he'd been thinking about it for some time. "So what do you say we do our own Last Supper this evening, on me?"

'Abbey sort of looked at him with this glint in her eye; it was obvious she didn't believe this was something he had planned. But I think by then she was happy to have Russ and me separated.

"Are you sure?" was all she asked him.

'That night we went to a place on the Viale Coni

Zugna — we'd been travelling cheap and wanted to treat ourselves. Russ was catching a late train and our plan was to eat and then walk him to the train station. But when Abbey and I ordered, he stood up and went to the counter.

'When he came back, he said. "It's all paid for kids, enjoy." He stuck his hand out and I shook it. He was smiling, and I realised he was happy for me. Abbey looked shocked, disappointed too; they'd been friends for years and you could see that things had changed between them now.

"You're a shit, Russ," she said as she hugged him.

"I know, but you love me anyway."

'And that was it. He went, and we sat there not knowing how to talk to each other. I wanted to comfort her, but I didn't know how.'

*

'We spent a few more days in Milan. We went to the Sforza Castle, Milan Cathedral, and visited all the small galleries. Abbey was quiet, I knew she was waiting for something from me.

'On our last day in Milan, after we'd eaten lunch we were sitting on the grass in Parco Sempione. The day was beautiful — the sky clear and the sun warm. Abbey was leaning on my shoulder, quiet but relaxed, and I told her about home. Once I started, it became easier. She didn't move her position, but reached for my hand and squeezed it. Her hair was tickling my cheek and her scent was intoxicating.

'I told her everything. I must have spoken for three hours and she never moved. When I finished, she hugged me; there were tears rolling down her face, but she was smiling. She was sad about everything I had said, but happy that I had confided in her.

'After that our relationship became easier. We travelled to Como, then on to Venice and Pisa and at the end, Rome. We never spoke about what would happen after Rome, we never considered what it would be like to face saying goodbye to each other.'

Cathryn stood up and adjusted her seat. She looked pensive; her eyes a little bloodshot.

'So what happened?' she asked. 'You didn't part company. You told me already you ended up in Exeter?'

'It was to be our last day,' I answered. 'Abbey's flight to Capetown was leaving the next day. I had no plan other than to stay in Rome a while longer and then go back to Manchester. That night we went to the Trevi Fountain. It was another warm, beautiful day. I told Abbey to have a glass of wine with dinner if she wanted to, but she refused. She told me she didn't need to drink to feel good and I thanked her.

'The Trevi Fountain was so unlike the other things we had seen in Rome, it has this ... pagan feel about it and at night with the light and shadow it's animated. All around us, young people, couples, were holding hands, hugging. I will not lie to you, my heart was breaking. I was deeply in love with Abbey and didn't want to lose her.

'She was beside me, holding my hand, her face sad. I pulled her towards me and looked into her eyes.

"I love you." It was the first time I'd said it. Not only to her, but to anyone. I think up to then, I didn't understand what love was or how to express it.

'She was smiling at me and crying, I could feel her body trembling against mine, the heat of her against my chest and I never wanted to let her go.

"I love you too."

'It felt ecstatic, to love and be loved in return.

"Don't go." She was still crying but laughing, and looking at me as if there was no one else in the entire world.'

*

I realise tears are streaming down my cheeks. I take a tissue from my pocket and wipe them away, embarrassed. But Cathryn's looking at me and smiling.

'Jesus!' I exhale.

'You really loved her?'

'Really.' I am getting control of myself or trying to.

'Ok. Our time is nearly up, but we'll come back to this. You have two questions.'

I'm glad to put memories of Abbey to one side. I know the first question I want to ask.

'Does Maria have a family?'

Cathryn thinks about this for a moment, then shrugs.

'Yes. She's not married — she doesn't believe in it, she's told me, but she's been with the same man for ten years. He's nice and treats her well. They have a daughter, she's eight years old. They call her Daniella.'

She smiles at this and I feel the tears threaten again. I've always been emotionally tough, but today I feel torn apart.

Cathryn looks at her watch. 'You have one more question.'

I speak on impulse. 'Why are you sad?'

Cathryn's eyes widen and her smile falters.

'That's not fair,' she whispers.

'I'm sorry, you're right. I shouldn't have asked.'

Small victories

When I leave Cathryn's office, I'm still immersed in memories. Maria named her child after me! I'm gripped with an eagerness to reach the end — and terrified I never will. I'm desperate to see her, and frightened that I might not.

'What is it you want from me?' I whisper.

A man walks past and looks at me, but I ignore him. I shove my hands into my pockets and walk. A memory surfaces unbidden: Abbey's face that last time. I push it away. Not today, I am raw with it. Keen to anchor myself, I think instead of Maria and our childhood.

*

I recall our voices — laughter, and a sweet aroma. Maria had stolen a bag of sugar and used it to make hard toffee. We ran around the house opening every door and window, but still the smell lingered.

'Ma will be back soon!' My voice was giddy with fear, but I was laughing.

Maria was too.

We'd struck back — regained our childhood for a sweet moment.

'The fire!' Maria grabbed me. 'If we light the fire, it'll get rid of the smell.'

I nodded wildly in agreement. It was frosty; Ma would not be cross.

I smile at the memory. It has lifted my mood.

Our luck held.

*

'I used a spoon full of sugar to get the fire going,' Maria confessed to Ma.

Ma sniffed and tutted in annoyance, and we hid our smiles.

It was a rare thing to beat Ma, but each small victory lifted us and made us feel whole again.

*

Happier , I cross the street and walk by railing of the park. I hear the sound of a child , screaming, not in pain but in joy, and laughter is coming through the shrubbery.

On impulse I enter the park. It's bright and cool and at its centre is the source of the laughter: a small girl on a swing, her mother pushing her. The girl's face is bright, her laughter unrestrained. I watch for a minute and then the mother turns towards me. She frowns, a look of concern in her eyes. I smile and continue my walk, not wanting to disrupt the moment.

The park is silent; I amble on and enjoy the peace.

Another memory surfaces.

*

Outside, summer rain beat on the tiled roof and rivulets smeared the window, painting the yard outside in surreal streaks, merging edges and blurring colours.

After she changed, the only game Maria played was Snap. We played it for hours and, though I tired of it, Maria never grew impatient with the tedium and predictability, and so I played because it was a way of connecting to her. Maria always won, though I didn't let her. I might have, if she had been struggling, but she was an expert at Snap. With her emotionless face and unfocused eyes, Maria predicted the fall of the cards, and slapped her hand on them before they settled. Then she'd whisper 'snap', her voice low, her eyes only on the cards, never on me.

She didn't smile or celebrate her win. And when the game was over, her hands moved rapidly, tidying the cards and replacing them in their box before putting them in my hands. Then she'd go back to the kitchen and continue with her work. She never spoke to me, and I grieved for my silent sister.

*

I blink the memory away, and I remind myself that Maria is no longer trapped in her Elsewhere. She is alive and happy; she has a daughter and she gave her my name.

I hunger for that thing that she has sent me in search of — her company, her smile, and the love which I have missed so much.

My leg is feeling stronger, and I walk on towards home.

When I arrive at the studio, the answering machine is blinking, and I play the message.nye.

'Hi, Dan.' It's Tiffany's voice. 'Cathryn wants you to come in on Wednesday morning. Call back if you can't make it, otherwise just be here for 9.15 am. Bye.'

*

On Wednesday morning I walk all the way to the

city. My leg is stronger, and for the first time I leave the crutch behind. It's an act of rebellion; I've been reliant on some form of crutch for too long.

It's growing colder, and a fine mist is blowing in off the bay. I turn my face up, welcoming the cool touch on my skin. The streets are still empty, the sound of a train echoes in the distance, and overhead gulls are drifting in the grey. I walk along the north circular road, through avenues of houses of fading grandeur. The trees are turning, the leaves drying, and the colours of autumn — yellow and vermillion and red — are visible among the green.

I leave Dorset Street and turn towards Cathryn's office. My breath is steady and my leg feels fine. I am buoyed up by optimism, and take the stairs without thinking.

As I climb, I am joined by two office workers, their obligatory coffee cups wafting steam that smells rich. I nod and they nod back as they turn towards offices on to the first floor. I continue to the second floor alone.

Tiffany greets me with a smile. 'You look well this morning, Dan.'

'Why, thank you!' My mood is ebullient; the walk has energised me. It's a small victory and I am eager to carry on.

'Cathryn will be free in a moment. She's just with someone.'

I nod, take a newspaper and sit down. The headlines are about tribunals; I flick through them idly, content to allow my mind to wander. The door to Cathryn's office opens, and a man walks out. This time I recognise Michael Grant. He looks ruffled; his hair is askew and his jaw is jutting out.

I catch sight of Cathryn as she closes the door behind him. She looks sad, or angry — it's hard to tell.

Tiffany calls goodbye after Grant but he ignores her. I glance up; he's looking at me. He says nothing and I turn away. My good humour evaporates. There's a click, the opening and closing of an aperture, a moment frozen: something changes.

*

Ten minutes later, Cathryn reappears and ushers me into her office.

'Hi, Dan,' she smiles. 'No crutch this morning?'

'No, I decided it was time.' I smile, though I'm unsure if I am talking only of the crutch.

I sit as she moves around the desk and faces me. She looks anxious. Her face is freshly scrubbed, but I think she's been crying — there is redness about her eyes. I want to ask why, but I have already pried too much.

'This morning I want to go back to the house.'

'Fine.' I'm glad not to talk about Abbey.

'You left the hallway where your parents' rooms were and walked back to the family room.'

Again I nod.

'What happened next?'

I drop my head, recalling the events now a week old.

'I was exhausted, but knew that if I was to climb the stairs, I would have to do it soon. My leg was aching and the drugs wouldn't have kept me upright for much longer.'

Cathryn nods for me to continue, but I am not ready yet. I take a deep breath and consider where I am and how I arrived here.

*

My body broke when it hit the concrete. But I hadn't killed myself. I'd failed at something so easy, and now I realise that I am glad. I'd stepped off a ledge, but I'd survived. I'd fractured my pelvis, both legs, arms and ribs. I'd smashed my wrists and shattered my cheekbones — but I had not severed my spine or damaged my brain.

When I woke, I was in the ward that became my home for the next three months. And on a floor full of people with broken bodies, I learned that others were suffering too; I wasn't alone. I healed, and the healing was more than physical — I'd rediscovered my will. Now that I've met Cathryn, I'm thankful, not only because I'm rediscovering Maria, but also because Cathryn too has become important.

I'm thinking how to answer her question, and I believe that I am as near to happiness as I have been in a long time. I will slay my own dragons and I know that she will help me.

Alcohol and self-loathing had waltzed me to the edge of that building, and memory was the hand that pushed me. Here in this room, with this woman, I believe I will find a way back. She is waiting for an answer.

I draw a breath and begin the journey again.

Sights and scents

'The stairs were narrow. Da called them the backstairs, only there were no front stairs in our house. They were wide enough for one person only, and even at that, you had to be careful. The bannister rail was low. I used to think that if I tripped, I might fall and it would collapse; I would imagine tumbling to the flags below and smashing my head, but now as an adult I see the fall is not so far.'

Cathryn responds with an encouraging smile.

'Our bedroom wasn't a bedroom at all. We called it the loft — it was an unconverted attic, a low space between the ceiling and the roof, with chipboard nailed onto wooden spans to form a base. Light shone between the cracks, and if I lay on the floor and peered through, I could see the rooms beneath. The roof was bare sheeting; it froze in winter and was too hot to touch in summer.

There was no insulation — it was damp and unhealthy.

'But it was ours, a space that Ma never entered. She was fearful of it, ashamed, and so she didn't acknowledge it.'

I visualise the grimness. I collect my thoughts, trying to explain.

*

'It was our sanctuary,' I begin. 'We spent the happiest times of our childhood there.'

I recall reentering it, my feet on the bare boards, my adult weight causing them to sag.

'I stepped through the opening — no door ever hung there. It shocked me how small it was. It appeared bigger when I was a child.'

I pause. 'Da avoided the loft too. The guilt of seeing where his children slept tortured him and so he did what he always did — he ignored it, pretending it didn't exist.'

'It sounds grim.' Cathryn frowns, imagining it.

But it wasn't always grim, as I tell her.

'Maria kept it neat. She hung pictures on the wall — found or made mats and rugs for the floor. She brought warmth and life to it, made it comfortable. Maria was a recycler. She salvaged things, cleaned and mended them, and breathed new life into them.'

Cathryn is nodding and a faint smile curves her lips. I imagine that what I have said resonates with her own experience of my sister. I'm envious of her relationship with Maria. I think of the woman in the picture, the older Maria whom I have not yet met, and then remember Maria as a child, and how for a long time her presence made that space a fortress. That place where, more than any other, we were children. Before she retreated into herself, Maria, brave and determined, was intent on making the most of what we had, always protecting me.

'At the back of the attic was a shelf,' I continue. 'Maria had painted it light blue, the paint salvaged from God knows where. It was where we kept treasures — games Da had given us, sweets we'd robbed from an aunt on a Christmas visit, apples and pears pinched from the garden that Maria stored, wrapped under sheets to prevent them from rotting. Things that others might not have considered at all, to us were important. They were evidence that we fought back, that we stuck our tongues out at Ma. They were proof that our lives had meaning.'

Then I tell her what I saw when I entered.

'I feared my weight might bring the whole thing crashing down, but it didn't. I moved to the skylight. It was only a Perspex sheet, but it allowed natural light into the attic. I looked over the crumpled roofs of the building, the feather-house and the machine shed, and beyond them the farmyard and the open front of the barn. I saw the remains of mouldering bales, and that the barrier that fronted the pig pen had collapsed in on itself.' My voice trembles, but I close my eyes and continue.

'I saw the block and tackle, the chains Da used when he was butchering pigs. The rusted boiler, too, and its broken flue leaning sideways.'

Cathryn reaches out, her fingers touch my hand. I open my eyes and look into hers.

'Are you ok?' she asks.

I shudder, suddenly cold. 'Yes,' I say.

'Go on,' she urges.

'Beyond the barn were fields — two grass paddocks so overgrown that only the tops of the fence posts were visible. A length of rusted barbed wire poked from over the grass, snapped and turned towards the sky. Beyond them was the harbour. Boats, red and blue and yellow, small as toys. The bigger boats had left years ago, moved west, to the porcupine banks or south to richer waters, the biggest going as far as Africa.'

I imagine the men who took memories of the village, cliffs and people to the coast of Namibia, and shudder. I feel melancholy for something I never had, but Cathryn is waiting for me to continue.

'They'd moored The Mary J at the head of the harbour. She looked dejected, her sides etched with age and rust, her bow dipped towards the water in surrender. Her soul ... '

I look up, wondering if Cathryn understands that boats have souls, even those beached in the mire of shallow water. .

How could she know that the Mary J needs salt to live, and needs waves breaking before her in the way soil parts before a plough share? It's been twelve years and some months since they lost Paul overboard, since the Mary J has sat abandoned, lifting and dropping on the highest tides only, living her half-life, her keel buried in black harbour mud.

Cathryn says nothing, allowing me time.

'I turned away and moved to the back window. The view was of the garden, overgrown. An apple tree grew there, its gnarled branches curled inward, resembling the fingers of a clenched fist, defying anyone within to dare emerge into sunlight. The outhouse was leaning over, the corrugated iron of the roof rusted and collapsed in on itself. I turned back to the room. The bed that was mine has collapsed, its base rotten. But Maria's bed was still intact, her pillow still lay where it always had, faded and damp.'

Cathryn is looking at me.

'I picked it up and held it to my face. It still held a memory of her — carbolic soap, and the scent that was just Maria, warm and soft. I hugged it as if I was hugging her, sitting on her bed, hoping it wouldn't give way. I wanted to stay there, to forget everything else ... '

I blink, clenching my fists, and biting back emotion,.

Cathryn's hand reaches out once more, her cool fingers brushing the back of my hand. 'Do you need a break?'

I exhale and nod.

*

Cathryn leaves me alone, but I'm still wrapped in the past.

I lay on Maria's bed, never wanting to leave, and clinging to the images of how we fought back. Memories of rebellion, our weapons — apples, pears and toffee.

But everything changed when Maria retreated into herself. I thought I was alone, that I had lost my sister. But Maria was stronger than any of us knew; she didn't care about herself, only about me. And she is alive, she survived.

I had one last place to visit: the back kitchen. Something was waiting for me there, but I was too tired and dizzy -. I dozed, the half-remembered scent of my sister on my skin and in my nose, and tears leaking from my sore eyes.

*

Cathryn returns with a tray.
'Coffee?'

I look up and smile at her, realising that she now knows more about me than anyone else, she knew more even than Abbey, and Abbey knew almost everything.

All the doubts I'd had — the opening of myself for inspection, revealing the damage — she'd made it tolerable.

She ushers me to the sofa.

'Will I be mother?' She blushes. 'Oh shit, what am I saying?'

I laugh at her embarrassment; she laughs too, and throws her head back, her eyes dancing. I think this journey is cathartic for her too — and I am glad.

Failure to engage

'You asked me what made me sad the last time we spoke,' Cathryn says.

I sit back and look at her, but she doesn't meet my eyes.

'I apologise for not answering. You've been honest with me, and I owe you the same.'

'You owe me nothing.' I reach out to touch her arm, and she turns towards me. Her eyes are wide with expectation — of what? I take my hand away.

'Our relationship is not one of doctor and patient.' Again she looks away. 'I'm not even sure how to define it, but I am glad that we are doing this.'

I make to answer her, but she turns back towards me.

'I'm glad,' she repeats, 'not because we are doing this for someone we care deeply for, but because it has allowed me to meet you, to get to know you.'

Her mouth twitches.

'I'm glad too … ' I mumble. I'm lost; I can't find the words I need.

She's looking at me, waiting, and her shoulders slump.

'I'm awful at this,' I say, taking her arm, trying to be what she expects.

She looks at me, her eyes downcast.

'What makes me sad,' she says, 'is that no matter how I try, I disappoint the people I love.'

'God, no!' I grip her arm tighter. 'You don't.'

'I do.' She reaches for a tissue. 'I've let Jen down — she has every reason to love her father; he's good to her, and good with her.'

'What's all this about, Cathryn?' I move closer.

'He's leaving, and Jen blames me.'

'Why … why does she blame you?'

'Because she's fourteen, and she only understands the things that affect her; she doesn't understand that parents can drift apart. She doesn't see that I have tried to keep it together, to overlook his oh-so-public affairs, his betrayal and disloyalty.'

She dabs at her eyes. 'I threw him out! The last time he was leaving to go back to Chelsea, I confronted him and the bastard grinned while he admitted it.'

'Are you sorry?' I ask, my hand still on her arm.

She shakes her head.

'No, but now Jen isn't talking about it, won't talk with me at all. She blames me and I can't help feeling that I failed her — failed all of us. My father went through hell to keep us all together when my mother died, but I couldn't. I've fucked up, and all I can think of is how Dad would handle it. He would have stayed.'

'No, he wouldn't.' I place my hand on hers. 'He wouldn't stay with someone who was cheating. Not if he's the man you told me he was.'

She's drying her eyes and looking at me.

'You've done the right thing.'

'Do you think so?' she sniffs.

'I'm sure.'

'Thank you.'

She smiles, but her eyes are full of her hurt and I let the moment slip away when I might have said more.

The hour is over.

*

Words form in my mind but, like water held back by stones, they stall, or come out in a rush and choke me; I can't sort them out as they parade through me. I leave Cathryn's office realising I've failed her. Everything I rely on flows from her — this journey she's guided me on, this essential submersion. Without her, I am lost. If I try alone, I'd drown, perhaps stand on a ledge again, staring down at a city festooned with lights, or a burning sky when day is born, or fading. Without her hand to pull me back, I would fall.

*

She is my salvation, in more ways than one. But I am as a hungry man who, when offered food, draws back for fear of what acceptance might cost. I have always been the hound snapping at the hand which reaches forth in kindness.

I slouch back towards my lair like a wounded animal, relishing new scars to slaver over, more misery to hide me from the world, and masks — bulwarks I've built to cower behind, believing myself safe from life, and from living.

*

In the mist curling in off the sea, I see faces form, each overlaid by others. Maria's first — the sister I did not protect. Had I muted the instinct to cherish her — Maria, whom I loved more than any other?

Maria who surrounded me like a fortress, her thin arms wrapping about me, her hair falling over me like a curtain, hiding me from Ma's fists and claws?

Mist falls on my cheeks and it stings.

I've built my fortress well, piling spite on denial, but Cathryn has breached it all and now it holds back nothing. I am back where it all fell apart.

I think of Abbey, her face dissolving into despair, her eyes fearful, but of what? I know the answer: of me, my voice, and my own burning, unforgiving eyes.

I no longer deny the memories. Later I'll relate them to Cathryn if she still wants to listen.

Back at the studio, I pull the bed from the wall and fall on it as if it is the hard prie-dieu, and I am facing the confessor. But there will be no absolution; I have failed those who could grant me forgiveness.

In Rome, Abbey and I had made a pact. We sealed it in neon-green darkness. The water of the Trevi Fountain was our witness and the cost to each was a kiss.

Thorn beneath my skin

We settled in Exeter. Abbey enrolled in the university to finish her MA which she'd abandoned a year earlier to travel. She was twenty years old, and I was a few months short of twenty-two. We were in love. We were a couple — self-contained yet not introverted. Abbey gathered admirers; she drew young, beautiful people to her and, like birds, they flocked, swooped and dived along the tree-lined streets, the sun reflecting off their hair and cheeks .

And I moved with them — out of step, a shadow.

*

Abbey embraced life in all its many facets, and I reshaped myself for her daily. I loved how she held her face up to the rain or threw her arms wide on Dartmoor, embracing the wind so it would lift her to her tiptoes, her hair rising like fire above her face, her smile, a promise.

I loved her in her quiet moments, when she sat by a window, gazing out at nothing, her face serene. And the world loved Abbey, too. She was a perfect fit; she left no wrinkles, no creases. She arrived in a new place and it was as if she had always been there. Within a day, people called out her name, within a week they accepted her as one their own. She had no guile, no backdoors, no secret caves. And I … I basked in her light.

We were in love. I have to believe that. But I had no map to guide me; I was like a ship floundering, drawn by the tide, but never sure how to maintain my heading. And when the wind changed, I was unprepared.

*

While Abbey threw herself into this new adventure, I drifted and procrastinated. I looked at courses I might attend, at careers I might pursue, fluttering like a moth drawn to a candle, hesitating, retreating from the heat, and questioning my own worth. But I never misled Abbey, except in one thing. I'd told her about my past — my childhood, Maria, Ma, all of it — opened myself to her as I had never opened myself to anyone. And she was gentle with me. She knew, without my ever telling her, how broken I was. But while she did nothing to damage me further, she also could not fix me.

I hid my addiction, and as she soared into a life made for her, I slid back into the life I thought she had saved me from. Was it an omen that they called the bar The Ship? Should I have fled? Yes.

When I told Abbey I'd found a job, she smiled. When I told her what it was, she still smiled, she hugged me and told me how proud she was, but I saw the fear in her eyes, and swore I would not hurt her.

*

On weekdays, I worked mornings in The Ship, and fell back into the life I was familiar with. I walked with Abbey to the university, kissed her beneath the arched branches of ancient trees, and then ambled along the river, dressed and ready for work. At first it was fine, I resisted urges which surfaced. I was young, strong and in love; I believed myself untouchable—that was my undoing.

*

The thing you think you have relinquished sits like a thorn under the flesh of your thumb. You scratch at it, forget it, sometimes gnaw at it, then put it aside again; you think you have exorcised it, but you have not!

Every day I faced it: regarded it from a safe distance, stepped back, and then approached it again, staring at it from the corner of my eye, turning my head so it faded. But it didn't fade, it grew bigger, until the thorn became a torment of itching and gnawing.

*

One drink — I told myself that I could handle it, I was strong, one drink would not dint my armour. I convinced myself that because I had survived once, I would survive again. And in fairness to myself (though I deserve no such fairness), I resisted for over a year.

I came home each day, stripped off clothes stinking of beer and spirits, held them to my nose and told myself how vile the stench was. Every afternoon I walked to the university, and I waited for Abbey. We kissed beneath the trees and linked hands; we strolled along the banks of the Exe and we spoke about the future.

In the evening, Abbey studied while I read. We

didn't own a TV. Abbey accepted this new life, and I convinced myself that I shared it. At night, we lay in each other's arms, exhausted from our love. This was our life, and the future stretched out before us, full of possibilities.

I succumbed. It's never one, but you convince yourself it will be. Then you have another one, and a pattern emerges.

*

Abbey forgave me; she did it with hurt in her eyes. She didn't ask me to stop; she didn't ask for anything. I told her it was not a big deal, that I was fine and in control — it was only a drink.

I told her she had strengthened me; I placed that burden on her shoulders, and felt a shift, like the altering of the tide, her flowing and me ebbing. Could I have changed? I don't know. I loved Abbey, but something else had a grip of me, something stronger than love. She didn't leave me; it was I who left. I ran from a vision of myself that loomed up from the past.

*

The wind changed to the northeast, and the sky was dark with thunderheads. I was drunk, not fall-down stupid drunk, but my head was buzzing, my blood popping and fizzing; I was alert, but not alert enough to sense the sadness in Abbey. She sat at the window, her books on the table in front of her, unopened. Her hands in her lap. She didn't look up; she didn't smile.

'We need to talk.' Her voice was so soft, I trembled.

I sat down opposite her and reached for her hands,

179

but she drew them back. Her eyes were shining with unshed tears. I tried to smile, but a sense of foreboding numbed me.

'I'm pregnant.'

When she said it, something burst inside me, like a flower blossoming in my chest, and for a moment I was delirious with happiness. I wanted to tell her how much I loved her; I wanted to hug and kiss her and tell her how happy I was. But she was crying.

'That's great!' I said.

She shook her head. 'It's not great, Dan. It's awful, it's inconceivable.'

'Why?' I asked. 'It's a baby, you'll be a mother, we'll be parents — a family.'

Abbey blinked. 'No, we won't be great, we'll be shit. I'll be sad, you'll be you. We can't.'

'What are you saying?' I tried to keep my voice level.

She was shaking her head again.

'I can't do this. You're not ready, Danny.'

'So … it's me.'

She looked up at me, her face contorted in grief.

'So what will you do?' I asked.

'You know.' She didn't want to say it, and the image of my mother clawed behind my eyes.

I called her a coward, a murderer; I stormed and raged, and she accepted it all. My words were sharp as razors. I said unspeakable things, loudly. And her unresponsiveness tore at me; her refusal to acknowledge me was like a punch.

Then I had her arm, my fingers digging into her flesh, my other hand raised. She didn't flinch or look away, and her eyes — like Maria's — were on me.

I threw her down on the chair and left. I walked along the river for miles. By dawn I was on the moor, my heart twisted and my mind racing with anger, not at Abbey but at myself.

For one awful moment, I'd become the thing I hated most — I'd become the dragon. I stood on a steep tor, looking back towards the receding city. Our two years together seemed unreal to me; I felt like an imposter.

I walked back to the city.

*

It was Saturday morning. The storm had passed, but the one in my head went unabated. When I got to the house, it was empty. Abbey had removed all her clothes, stripped the beds.

There was no note, no goodbye, no asking forgiveness; she had nothing to ask forgiveness for.

Blood

At 7.30 pm. I phone Cathryn's number. I expect to get the machine, but she answers.

'We need to finish this.' I say

'Come in at eight o'clock tomorrow morning.' She sounds defeated, and I know she had expected more of me.

'Ok,' I answer, but she's already hung up.

*

It feels as though we're beginning again. The trust and familiarity, the relationship — however we'd defined it — has dissolved into nothingness. She doesn't mention the previous day, but the warmth that had grown between us is absent. I'd put up a wall and now I didn't know how to tear it down.

I focus only on getting this done, getting to whatever memory it is that I need to find and beyond that to find Maria, but beyond that again, I have no plan.

Cathryn looks at me.

'You lay down on Maria's bed, you held her pillow to your face.'

I nod and wait.

'What happened after that?'

'I must have fallen asleep,' I begin. 'I was woozy from the drugs or the pain. When I woke up, my mouth was full of fluff.'

'The kitchen was the last room — the kitchen and

the scullery,' Cathryn prompts me, eager to finish this and, I feel, to finish with me.

'Yes,' I answer. 'I sat up on Maria's bed, groggy, the floor swaying under my feet. I tried to stand, but had to sit down again. Standing was the hardest part but once I was upright, the lightheadedness subsided.

'I stood at the opening. The loft behind me was bright, the room below dim and dusty. I made my way down, putting the crutch in front of me at each step, letting it support my weight, so I didn't fall. The bloodstone stood at the entrance to the kitchen, smooth, worn down by our feet, by generations of feet. I imagine the feet of elder O'Neill and Ellis families passing over it and stepping into the small kitchen.

'I stood looking at it, my arms trembling and my breath coming in shallow heaves. I didn't know why it frightened me, but I was unsure if I had courage enough for this single step. My lips were quivering and I was mumbling, "say something, say something". I was speaking to the air.'

I fell silent, gripping the arm of the chair. Cathryn is looking at me.

'What were you frightened of?' Her voice is softer.

I shake my head. 'I don't know. Something happened there, in the kitchen, something awful.'

'Tell me.'

*

'I placed the tip of the crutch on the bloodstone and stepped up, vaulting almost, not wanting to stand on it. Then, one more step, and I was in the kitchen. It was tiny. Light spilled in through the cracked window

183

and leaves that had blown in decayed in the sink. The table was still there, the surface bleached by sun. Moss covered the floor, the roof was collapsing, and I could see the sky and gathering clouds. Beyond the window was a tangle that was once a garden; the pear tree was larger than I remembered, and its branches rustled in the wind. Shadows moved and shapes danced along the privet; it was wild and overgrown.'

'Was there anything else?'

'Yes!' My eyes fly wide open.

'What, Dan? What did you see?'

'Blood.' My voice cracked. 'I saw blood.'

*

Cathryn goes to the reception for a glass of water. I swallow it as if I'm parched. I taste the dust of the house on my tongue, on the roof of my mouth.

She sits down and looks at me.

'The blood you saw, was it real?'

'No, it was there for a moment, in the sink, on the walls, under my feet, slimy like I was standing on wet tiles — but the floor was dry, covered in dust and grit.'

'Was it a memory?'

'I don't know; it looked real. I stepped backward out of the kitchen, afraid to stay there, almost tripping on the bloodstone. I had to reach back with the crutch to balance myself.'

'And then?'

I grunt, embarrassed.

Cathryn is looking at me.

'I ran,' I shrug. 'Backed out of the house and ran, hobbled away. And now, I have to go back.'

I sit in silence: it was all for nothing. A gasp rises from my chest, a knot of fear, choking me. Cathryn reaches out her hand and I grasp it; this time I don't let go, trying to communicate everything in that one touch. She stands, comes rounds the desk, and takes my head against her breast. I sob like a child, her hands on my hair and the sound of her heart beating in my ear.

Learning to fly

Da survived for ten years, but his failure to protect his children became a disease that ate at him. He became a father too late. After, when he'd surrendered everything, he did all he could to protect me, but was powerless to change the past. But he shielded me from the future; he protected me from the awfulness of that day.

When I left, he gave up. He sat in that room that he never claimed as his own, waiting for the end, for death. In his final days he never left it; he didn't eat, didn't wash. The night he died, he stripped himself naked and lay on the bed, the windows open wide. It was March and outside it was snowing; the temperature had dropped to −10 Celsius. The autopsy recorded his death as natural, stating that he died of hypothermia compounded by poor nutrition; the implication was, that confused, he had left the window unfastened, or that the wind had blown it open. But I knew that wasn't true.

My father killed himself. He had starved himself for weeks before freezing to death, but not to prove a point, or because of past sins. It was not an act of contrition or protest: it was a surrender. He let himself die because he didn't care; he had nothing left. He died the day his son found blood all over the kitchen floor.

I was twenty-eight when Da died; the news came in an email from Paul. I missed his funeral because by the time I read the message it was a month old. Paul was not to blame. I'd cut myself off, email was the only way to contact me, and my life as it was then didn't lend itself to having access to a computer or smartphone.

When I learned of his death, I returned to Dublin.

I went to visit the grave. I told no one and made no plans to stay. In the graveyard I stood before the marker and read the inscription, his name, the years and the epithet 'Husband and father'. I didn't laugh, nor cry, though afterwards I wished that things had been different between us.

They buried him in a new plot, one he'd bought himself; the planned final resting place for all his family became a sad shrine to a life ended alone. He'd been dead since the moment he lost Ma; he loved her.

I didn't pray, I'd forgotten how to. Ghosts hovered close. I walked to the crossroads and waited for two hours in the bitter cold, huddled and hidden beneath a parka, the hood wrapped tight, showing only my eyes. I waited to leave and assured myself I would never return.

*

At forty-three years old, I jumped from a balcony. For over half my life I'd struggled with addiction and nightmares, with fear, paranoia and depression. I'd tried to forgive myself, but I couldn't.

I left Da looking for a new life, but I'd never escaped the life I left in the village. It pursued me across Europe, and I came back.

George

Cathryn calls me early on Friday morning.

'Can you come over tonight?' She sounds excited.

'Yes,' I answer, wondering why. 'Where?'

'My house. Come for about 7.00. No — make it 6.00. Have dinner with us.'

'Ok, but why?'

'Don't worry.' Her voice is light, playful. 'It's just dinner, and I have something for you!'

There's a fluttering deep in my stomach as I jot down her address.

*

I spend the day in the city. First, I go to the barber's; I consider having my beard shaved off as the scar on my face is almost healed, but settle instead for a trim. For the next two hours, I forage through racks of cheap suits, disputing between casual or smart. I finally settled on slacks, a jacket, and a white shirt.

By four o'clock, I'm back at the studio, showered and dressed but it's too early to leave. I pick up a newspaper but discard it. I try reading a book but my mind will not settle. I can think only of Cathryn, and the evening ahead.

Since leaving Exeter, I've avoided any kind of relationship. I wonder now whether I'm ready, or whether I'm starting something that will lead to pain for both of us. Again, I think of the past.

*

It had been easy to fall. I had a reason, an excuse, and I blamed Abbey. Like both Ma and Da, I never acknowledged my own part, my own guilt. Abbey left because she saw what I was becoming. After she left, the slide into addiction was easy, comforting — a homecoming, almost. I lost my job, I'd become an unreliable employee who didn't turn up — or I turned up drunk, or drank while I worked.

It was autumn when Abbey left, and the weather was growing colder. By Christmas, I'd worn out the patience of the few friends I had. I carried my pain in rough shards, and became a belligerent drunk. In lucid moments, I looked in the mirror and saw my mother's eyes staring back at me. Self-hate was easy, but I was still some way from self-destruction.

I lived on the streets, odd jobbing or begging, and doing whatever I needed to feed my addiction. I ate only if I had money left over which wasn't often. I drank red wine, cider, sherry; the contents of the bottle became secondary to the release. Some nights the shelters would admit me if I got there dry. When I didn't, I slept in doorways, on park benches or under bridges, and often I woke not knowing or caring where I was.

I became a non-person, unseen by most. I was dirty, drunk, and often sick. Summer and winter I wore a long dark coat which I wrapped around me at night. I survived on the scraps that decent people gave me, or on those I found. In the fifth winter, I met a man who changed my luck and my life.

*

The lights of the trailer drew me to it, the aroma

of coffee, of soup and frying meat. Hunger gnawed at my guts and yet if I ate, I would not hold the food in my stomach. I hadn't eaten in two days and I had no money. I was in withdrawal, my body shivered with need, my hands trembled in my pockets.

The trailer was blue and white like the canopy that hung over it. As I drew closer, the torment of smells twisted my guts, my body reacting to a need while my mind rejected it. I walked towards it with no idea of what would happen when I got there.

I saw plastic tables out in front of the trailer, four chairs around each. When I reached the first, I stumbled, I grabbed for the table, missed it and fell.

'Hey, fella!' I heard a voice, high and angry. 'What do you think you're doing?'

I tried to stand by leaning on a table but my weight caused it to tilt and fall, and I fell with it.

'Ah, for fuck's sake!'

I heard a door open and close.

'Come on, lad, get up!'

Hands grabbed me and I flinched, expecting a punch or a kick. I curled up, protecting my head and my groin.

'Jesus, don't make it so hard, lad.'

The voice was gruff, but gentle. I looked up. The man was short and fat, and his face was soft, like a child's. He wore an apron and, on his head, what looked like a naval cap, the legend George's Place emblazoned across it.

George helped me to stand and then sat me on a chair while he straightened the table. I sat, only dimly aware of him. He put a Styrofoam cup in my hand. I reacted to the warmth, hunching over it. It was soup; I tried to swallow it, but I coughed and heaved. I leaned over and puked but there was nothing in my stomach.

'Easy, lad.'

He took the cup from me while I retched.

'Jesus, you have it bad, don't you?'

He waited until I sat straight again and then his fingers wrapped around mine, clamping them on the warm cup.

'Try again,' he said. 'Go slow this time.'

'I can't pay, I have no money,' I said, trying to hand the cup back to him.

'Do you think I don't know that?' He smiled, his cheeks red and round, dyed blond hair sticking out from under his jaunty hat.

'It's only soup, it won't bankrupt me.'

He left me sitting there, and as I sipped the soup, I noticed where I was — the carpark of a large pub. I saw lights shining from the windows and the entrance. It was late, people were leaving and soon a queue of them were talking to George and ordering food. The aroma of chips frying, the tang of tomato sauce and onions both attracted and repulsed me.

Later, when there was a lull in the queue, he brought me more soup and I thanked him. I wanted to do more; it had been a long time since anyone had shown me kindness.

'Take it slow, and then we'll see about feeding you.'

He left me again, and I looked about. People were standing, eating burgers and chatting in groups —

they looked so normal. I felt ashamed to be among them and wanted to leave, but I didn't. George had a gas heater near the trailer and though I wasn't close to it, the light warmed me.

When the last of the people disappeared, after I heard George moving in the trailer, closing flaps, rearranging things, he came and sat beside me. He put two burgers wrapped in tissue on the table and two plastic trays with fries.

'So, what's your story, lad?'

I ate both burgers and spoke between mouthfuls; I told him more than I intended to. He sat quietly, nodding but without interrupting; it was like I was talking to the night, to the moon. The words spilled from my mouth, and I told him about my pain, Abbey, everything. When I finished, he considered me.

'Have you got a licence?'

The question was so unexpected that I thought I'd misheard him.

'What?'

'A driving licence?'

I rifled through my pockets, drew out a leather case and handed it to him.

My licence was still valid, but I hadn't driven in four years.

George looked at it, his lips moving silently as he read my name. He looked at me, comparing the photo to the ragged man I was, and nodded, satisfied.

'OK, Daniel. Do you want a job?'

I was incapable of answering, but nodded, and he smiled.

'We'll get you cleaned up so.'

*

George was overweight, gay, frumpy, but he had more heart and courage than anyone I'd ever met. From the outset, he was under no illusions about me. He understood what I was. He didn't ask me to stop drinking; he was wise enough to know I wouldn't. But he ensured I was upright and sober each morning. And when I wasn't, he huffed and puffed, but he got by without me. Afterwards, when he'd bawl at me and I'd apologise, I worked harder to make up for letting him down.

At first, I slept at George's house and later, when I had a little money, I rented a room in the city.

*

Over almost two decades of summers, we travelled to countless events all around Devon and Cornwall — music events, horse shows and fetes — and in winter we flipped burgers and fried chips. We spent hundreds of hours on the road and thousands more working together, and became friends. It didn't happen straightaway. He scolded me, threatened me, cajoled me and swore he would fire me, but never did. And slowly we became more than friends, we became a family — and laughed a lot.

In those first years, I still drank every day, but I worked, ate daily and became more dependable. I became what I had been at twenty years old, a functioning alcoholic. Later, I went through phases of trying to quit. George was fractious, but supportive. His stories, his camp humour and his attitude rubbed off on me. He was sarcastic, funny and irrepressible. At full flight he could handle loads of people queuing at the hatch, entertaining them as he fed them. People liked George for his spirit, his kindness and his irreverence.

I loved George. I also knew, once he came to rely on me, that if I truly fucked up, he'd sack me. He was sentimental to a point, but he was serious about business.

'It's what feeds us, lad,' he'd say, pointing at the trailer, the fryers, the fridges. The truth, when I consider it, is that George saved my life.

*

On the twenty-eighth of November 2016, George was working alone. It was a Monday, a slow night, and after I'd helped him set up, he worked alone. I'd been clean for three months and that night, I went to a club to watch a local band. I told George I'd come later to help him with the clean and close. The 'C'&'C' he called it every night.

But George closed early. There was a strange crowd in the pub; they had come down to attend a political rally, and they spooked him. He'd already hitched the trailer to his old Land Rover defender and was pulling down the shutter when two men came out of the pub laughing and joking.

Something in their manner scared George. He could deal with idiots and smart-arses. Rowdy drunks and homophobic insults were nothing new; we met and handled them daily, and George deflected them with a quip or a burger.

Witnesses said, George was inside the trailer when they rapped on the shutters. He didn't answer, perhaps he hoped they would go away, but they didn't. Instead they knocked harder, and when he still didn't answer they rocked the trailer, banging on it and pushing it. When George called to them to stop, they rocked it harder. The fryers were still scalding hot when the first one tipped and the hot oil spilled over the floor of the trailer.

The two men continued rocking the trailer and others came to join them. Two local men who knew George tried to stop them, but the louts turned on them. One ran back inside and called the police. The other saw the trailer set alight and the flames spreading fast, and the bastards who surrounded it fell back and then ran. Four gas cylinders in the trailer rumbled one after the other and the trailer exploded.

The police found George's burnt body where it landed in the scrub behind the pub carpark. By the time I arrived, there were cops everywhere. The heat had twisted the Land Rover and the trailer to steel skeletons.

I stood there, numb. It was raining, and I was wearing only a tee-shirt and jeans. The police questioned me, and I mumbled answers.

*

I left Exeter after the funeral and returned to Dublin. A month later I was on a ledge, drunk, looking down over a city strewn with lights. I saw something that night. But I missed something too; I stepped forward too early. I wonder if I can find it again — and what damage it might cause if I do.

Images

I drive out of town well beyond the city limits. Her home is on the edge of a stretch of woodland that straddles the border of Dublin and Kildare. The sky is already dimming when I arrive.

The house is in the centre of a block of three bungalows, all walled off, on large landscaped plots with gravel drives. I check the number on the pillar and drive in.

Cathryn's daughter answers the door.

'Hi.' She flicks her hand up in a perfunctory greeting, and holds the door as I step into a hallway neither large nor extravagant. The walls are painted and the wooden floors are covered with scatter rugs, Cathryn's influence clear in the muted greys and autumnal browns and reds.

Jen walks ahead of me and leads me to a large kitchen where Cathryn is working over a stove.

'Hi!' she greets me. 'Dinner will be ready in about ten minutes, so I hope you brought your appetite.'

'I'm starving!' I smile to hide my nervousness.

Jen disappears through an open door and flops down in a chair, a TV remote in her hand.

'Is your homework finished?' Cathryn asks her.

Jen rolls her eyes. 'Yes, mum.'

*

I lounge against the kitchen cabinets and watch Cathryn working. She's wearing baggy jeans and a pink sweatshirt, and her hair is pulled back from her faced. I'm struck by the simple domesticity; it's strange to me, yet I find it achingly comfortable — though I'm still not sure why I am here.

Dinner is a rack of lamb, crusted with garlic and served with baby roast potatoes and roasted vegetables. The smell as Cathryn takes it from the oven is rich and aromatic, and I am reminded how long it has been since I last ate a home-cooked meal.

Cathryn calls Jennifer and I feel suddenly nervous sitting down to eat with them. I'm mindful of what Cathryn has told me about Jennifer blaming her for her father's absence, and wonder how she feels about having a strange man in the house for dinner.

As the girl takes her seat, I focus on my plate, avoiding her eyes.

'What! No wine?' She looks at her mother.

'No,' Cathryn replies. 'Dan doesn't drink alcohol.'

'Not at all, or not anymore?'

'Not anymore,' I say. I look at Jennifer and smile.

Her eyes glint. 'Is that why you see my mum? You're in recovery or something?'

'Jen,' Cathryn warns, but I cut across her.

'No, I see your mum because she is helping me find something I've lost, something important.'

'What?' The girl is looking at me. I turn to Cathryn, but she is dissecting the lamb.

'I had a sister, she was about your age.' My palms are sweating. 'Something happened, something I've forgotten. Your mum is helping me remember, helping me to find my sister.'

Jennifer opens her mouth to speak .

'Your mum is an incredible woman,' I say quickly. 'She has no reason in the world to help me, and yet she's doing it.'

I hold Jennifer's gaze and feel Cathryn's eyes on both of us.

'Will you find your sister?' Jennifer's voice is softer now, and curious.

'I think …' I falter. 'I hope so, with your mum's help. She's very kind.'

Jennifer smiles and looks at her mother. 'Yes, she is.'

I risk looking at Cathryn. She's fussing with the food, but her cheeks are flushed, and she's smiling.

'Come on, the food's getting cold,' she says, a little too loudly.

*

When we finish dinner, I help Jennifer clear the dishes and stack them in the dishwasher. She continues to question me, and I feel I'm being interrogated.

'Why don't you drink?'

I think for a minute and then opt for honesty.

'Because I'm an addict.'

'Why?'

Again, I hesitate, searching for an answer.

'My mother drank. She was an alcoholic; we didn't get on well, and I think I inherited something from her.'

'What about your father — was he an alcoholic too?'

'No, he wasn't.'

I wonder if she is about to say something about

her own father, but she just smiles. She stows the last of the dishes, then returns to the TV room, remote in hand, no longer interested in me. I heave a sigh of relief.

'Dan and I are just going to stay in here and talk,' Cathryn says.

Jennifer nods as her mother slides the door between the two rooms over.

She turned and mouths 'thank you' to me. I shrug awkwardly.

'I'm having a coffee. Do you want one?'

I nod and retake my seat, watching her as she fills the machine, sets the cups before it and then pours.

When Cathryn comes to the table, she's carrying a folder. She places the coffee down and sits close. Her perfume and her nearness are unnerving; I'm unprepared for this intimacy, yet I crave it.

'I want to show you these.' She opens the folder and spreads out a stack of prints. 'They're not the originals,' she explains.

They are charcoal sketches, each wrapped in tissue. I unwrap the first one . It shows Da, standing beside a car, arms folded and his sardonic grin are both unsettling and life-like. Gráinneog sits by his feet. Cathryn says nothing, but she places her hand on my arm. The second depicts Ma, standing by the kitchen door, arms folded across her chest, eyes distant. But the one I'm drawn to is the third one. It shows Maria and me sitting by the fence that divides the two fields; Maria is leaning towards me, her mouth by my ear, whispering something. I'm looking straight ahead, smiling, my eyes drawn in exceptional detail. Below the sketch is a title, 'Secret' and Maria's signature.

My hands go from one to another, touching them, each sparking memories.

Cathryn's squeezes my arm. 'She drew them from memory.'

She picks up the one that I had been examining. 'This she drew only a couple of weeks ago. I wonder what the secret was. Do you remember?'

I nod, and smile. I hear her words like the susurration of wind through a meadow: 'I'll never leave you.'

I turn away, hiding my emotion.

'Maria wants you to have these,' Cathryn says, gathering them up and replacing them in the folder.

'But there are more?' I ask.

She opens an envelope and places four more sketches on the table. They are not prints this time, and they have no titles or signature. I pick up the first image. In it, I am lying on the sofa. A second figure is leaning over me, her hair cascading down around my face. And now I remember her, standing like that, whispering something in my ear, but I don't remember her words.

I examine the next sketch, the Mary J drifting at sea. It's night, and two figures stand on the deck — Uncle Paul, cloth cap pulled down, and the second a girl, hair blowing in the wind. A memory stirs, faint as a light flickering at the corner of my vision that disappears when I turn towards it.

The third image is a simple drawing, rather bleak, the details of the barn shaded in. But in the centre is the block and tackle, the chains dangling, and behind them the glowing grate of the boiler. I shudder, the memory coalesces, and I push it back.

Cathryn places her hand on my shoulder, and I recoil in fright. She moves closer. 'It's ok,' she whispers.

I reach to reveal the final page, but I hesitate. Something is gathering, like darkness surrounding me. I lift the page. The final image is not black but red — a bloody handprint. I flinch and Cathryn wraps an arm about me.

'I'm sorry,' she whispers. 'I'm sorry.'

I re-stack the images, so they are back in order. The sketch of Maria leaning over me is on top.

'What are these?' My voice is ragged.

'They are Maria's memories of that day,' Cathryn says. She is still standing beside me, her hip against my shoulder, and I dread her moving away.

'She thinks they will help.'

I shake my head. 'They don't,' I whisper. 'I don't understand them — I don't remember ... '

'I can help you.' Cathryn is watching me, her eyes intent. 'If you want me to.'.

'How?'

'Regression,' she says.. 'I've only done it once before, and it's not an exact science but I think it might work for you. We can try it if you would like.'

'Yes,' I say, reaching out towards her as she takes my hand in hers.

'I want to remember ... ' I point to the pictures. 'It's the only way to end it.'

But I'm trembling, more frightened than I have been in years.

201

Back sliding

I drive home through heavy showers, the rain scudding sideways across the road in the wind, and the images Maria drew and her words 'I'll never leave you' repeating over and over in my mind.

She'd rendered me in minute detail, yet I struggle to recall her face.

I blink away the image of the bloodstained hand, but it forms again, and I realise it's not just an image, but a memory — Maria's memory, but one I share, and which terrifies me.

*

By the time I reach the city, I'm tired and emotionally exhausted yet terrified at the prospect of sleep. I pull into the parking space, get out and lock the car, but instead of turning towards my door, I turn back to the city. I walk towards the all-night shop, my hands buried deep in my coat pockets. I want to forget — to run. And I know what I will do.

That thing that drove me to the ledge is stalking me again, and I feel its fetid breath hot on my neck. My hands tremble as I walk, my leg aches for the first time in a week. I shake out my pocket, searching for pills that I know I don't have. I find only lint.

The lights of the store come into view and I walk faster, afraid of the encroaching darkness. I long for the light. My watch reads 9.15 pm and yet the cloud is so pervasive that it feels like the deadest hour of night. I focus on the lights until I step through the entrance of the shop, rain dripping off me.

Inside, the florescent lights buzz, and the pop and fizz in my blood is loud in my ears. I've already made my mind up, yet I turn elsewhere and walk the aisles. I'm too warm, and the food I'd eaten earlier lies like a weight in my stomach. I unbutton my coat and run a hand across my forehead; it comes away wet. I look at my fingers as though they are someone else's, from elsewhere. That's what Maria called the place she went to — Elsewhere. I need to go there now.

I turn from the bread and cereal to the back of the store. The wine is on short shelves — reds and whites, Merlot and Chardonnay — their silver and gold foil tops reflecting the light, their sloping shoulders curvaceous as a girl's hip. My hand tremors and my breath comes in a rush . I grasp the neck of a bottle without looking and pull it towards me.

The man at the counter is serving an old woman and I wait, bottle clasped to my chest. When my turn comes, I reach for my wallet. I hesitate before putting the bottle on the counter and my fingers are awkward as I pull out notes, and something flutters to the floor. The man is watching me, his eyes knowing; I try to smile, but he looks away. I find a twenty; he says something, but I don't understand, the roar in my ears blocking out every other sound. He hands me my change and I stuff the money into my coat pocket and walk back out into the darkness.

Fifty metres from the store I realise I am carrying the bottle in my left hand, unwrapped, the streetlights reflecting off the green glass. I stuff it into my jacket pocket, my hand still clasping it as a drowning man would a life buoy. I'm lightheaded, dizzy, on the brink of something dangerous.

*

I can't find the keyhole. My hand is shaking as I scratch the key over metal, and it skitters away. I pick it up, and this time it slides home, and I'm in. I lean against the wall, the wine still in my pocket, my fingers locked on the smooth glass. I wait for my breathing to slow, and only then do I turn on the lights.

The room looks different. The breakfast bar is too white, its edges sharp and details distinct — the three cabinets, white doors, one with glass, and behind the glass are plates and two mugs. One mug has something printed on it — a question mark and the word TEA. What does it mean? I try to focus, and to remember where the cup came from; it seems somehow important. But I can't; I shake my head and turn away.

I take the wine to the coffee table and brush the books to the floor, then take the envelope from my pocket. I spread the sketches out, looking away as I do so, reluctant to see them, yet my actions are independent of thought. My fingers are shaking as I unscrew the top of the wine and place the open bottle on the table between them. I don't bother with a glass.

Then I get to my feet, unsure what I am doing or why. I am standing outside myself, frightened. I lean against the wall, my fingers at my eyes, blocking out the light and everything. I slide to the floor and don't look up.

*

Time passes, but I don't know how much; the clock makes no sense. It reads 11:00 in flashing neon, but is it night or morning? Outside is dark — it must be night.

The wine bottle is still on the table and my chest constricts. I kneel up, terrified. I'm shaking, clenching my fist, and tears of anger and frustration wet my face. The sketches lie on the table. I stare at them. I pick up one, and see Maria leaning towards me, her lips to my ear, and again I hear the words, 'I will never leave you.' The sketch of Da lies sideways, his eyes boring into mine, and beneath it is Ma, her eyes squinting, cross. I reach out and draw it towards me, stare into those eyes. I imagine her voice, her anger. My fist closes around the image, the paper scrunching as I squeeze. I throw it from me. There's a taste in my mouth, sweet and acidic. I exhale, knowing I've lost. I glare at the wine bottle, hating how it seduced me, how I allowed myself to surrender to addiction.

Beside the bottle lies the picture of the bloody handprint. Something awful rises in me, curling inwards, and I want to lie on the floor and weep. Maria's voice echoes again, 'I will never leave you.' And I am raging, at Ma, at Da, and at my own weakness. I spit, a reflex. I see blood on my new shirt. It's flowing from my mouth, sweet and acrid. I spit into my open palm and see blood.

There's an audible click, a pause, and the pendulum swings again.

205

I pick up the wine bottle; it's still full.

My hand jerks back from it as though it's alive, like a snake ready to strike. I stand, staring at it, realising how close I've come. And now I hate it; I grab the bottle, holding the neck away from me as I drain the contents down the sink. I rinse it, but can still smell the wine, the sweetness. I take the bottle out into the night and stand in the side alley in my shirt; my front stained from the blood where I have bitten my own tongue. The rain is stronger, falling from every direction and the wind is howling, the trees along the roadway bowing in the gale.

*

I hurl the bottle at the wall; it explodes and the fragments scatter.

The metronome

Cathryn's eyes grow wide and I worry that she'll refuse to help me. I'm ashamed of how close I came, and terrified that it will all end here.

She remains quiet as I tell her, but her eyes never move from mine. I'm like a child confessing to a wrong and I want to look away, but the weight of her gaze will not allow it.

'You bought wine?' Her eyes are bright, forcing me to answer.

'Yes.'

'But, didn't drink it?' There is no hardness in her eyes.

I nod and shrug; I know how close I came.

'That's what's important, Dan — you didn't drink it.'

I nod agains., and she dismisses the subject.

'Let's move on.' She sits up straight, her eyes contemplative. 'It's important that you understand the process.'

I lean forward, excited and tremulous in equal measure.

'Regression is not an exact science — detractors say it's not a science at all. And I must advise, you may be prone to suggestion.'

She pauses. 'I also have to warn you that it might be dangerous.'

'How?'

She frowns. 'The mind is often thought of as fragile, but it's not, it's strong. It has its own defences. It often rejects things it can't contain and suppresses memories that might harm it. This is common in children, less so in adults.'

I nod my understanding.

'When we strip away that defence, in effect we are taking you back in time.' She points at me. 'You may relive — or recall — experiences that your mind suppressed. The danger inherent in the process is obvious. What we will hope for is that the memories you suppressed as a child will be tolerable for you as an adult, but we can't be certain.'

'You mean the memories might be too much for me, that they might make me crazier than I already am?'

'You're not crazy, Dan. Far from it, but yes, the memories might be too much, the emotion might overwhelm you, drive you … '

'To drink.'

She shrugs. 'It's a danger, yes.'

'But this is what Maria wants!' My voice is harsher than I intended.

Cathryn winces. 'She doesn't want to hurt you, Dan. I promise you that.'

'Do you know?' I ask, suddenly realising that she does, that this is what she has been guiding me towards.

'What?'

'You do, don't you?'

Cathryn blinks.

'You know what she wants me to remember, don't

you?'

'In part…but not all of it' She looks apprehensive. 'I can't betray a promise, please don't ask me to do that.'.

The anger drains out of me.

'I understand,' I say. 'Let's do it.'

*

I watch the metronome ticking, and feel my eyes grow heavy and I feel myself sinking as though into pillows. I hear Cathryn's voice, it's soft.

'What's your name?'

'Danny O'Neill.'

'What age are you?'

'I'm fourteen.'

'Where are you, Danny? Can you tell me what you see?'

*

'I'm in a field. Wind is bending the grass towards me and the paddock looks like the sea, waves forming as the wind whips through it. It's September, the grass is no longer green but turning yellow, seeding. It's too late to cut for hay, but after Ma killed the baby, Da was too sad to mow, to stand or sit, or even speak.

'Above me a storm is gathering. My skin is scratchy as though the energy of the storm is surging through me. The sun moves from behind a cloud and storm light makes everything stand out. The colours are bright and the shadows dark, enormous. I run towards the yard and Jess moves beside me; she scatters a group of hens; the rooster stands his ground, his red and orange plumage shimmering, his eyes dangerous.

'Wind whistles and rattles through the gaps of buildings. The yard is full of sounds, timbers creaking and roof sheets banging. Tendrils of ragged honeysuckle lift over the hen-house roof, and small birds — sparrows — fly over it, their wings fighting the wind. The clouds are low, so close I could touch them; they're dark and angry at the centre and at their edges, they are too bright to look at.

'A cat runs across the yard and into the machine shed, her back arched. She spits and hisses. And there are other sounds — voices, an argument, Maria screaming. I run, and the rain comes hard. It soaks my hair, and my tee-shirt sticks to my back. There's water in my eyes and on my lips, I can taste it. I hear Maria's scream again — I have not heard her voice in weeks.

'The Lady in the Glass reflects the dark sky, and as I reach the door, thunder explodes — a long sound, like rocks tumbling over a tin roof. I hear a dog bark, then another scream and I push the door, the wind catches it and slams it off the inner wall, loudly. I call Maria's name, but she doesn't answer; the house is silent. The floor is wet, and rain blows in from the open door.

'I run to the kitchen, frightened of the silence, but I hesitate, something smells bad, like offal or vomit.

'I jump across the black step and land on the linoleum of the kitchen floor, my impetus carrying me forward on the wetness. It's not rain — the rain cannot have entered this far. It is something else.'

*

I groan. The shock of it pulls me back. I am huddled deep in the chair, Cathryn is by my side, holding me close, hugging me and whispering. 'It's ok, I'm here.'

I sit up and hold her. And then I push her away, shaking my head.

'It was too soon.' I say urgently. 'I need to try again.'

'Let's wait.' She looks scared.

'No, I have to do it now.' I squeeze her arms, and she flinches. I release her.

'Please!'

Crossing the bloodstone

Cathryn gives me two tablets and a glass of water.
'They're mild, but they'll help you relax.'

Her brow is twisted in worry; I know she doesn't
want to do this anymore, it frightens her. But I'm
convinced that knowing cannot be worse than not
knowing, so can't turn away now.

I wash down the tablets with a sip of water, and
replace the glass on the table. Grasping Cathryn's
hand in mine, I close my eyes, waiting for the
sedative to work.

The metronome is ticking again, and I am sliding,
moving down.

*

'The floor is sticky … I see blood.'

I feel a scream that will not come. It's stuck deep
down, growing, but refusing to erupt — it's choking
me. But the warmth of Cathryn's hand anchors me.

I take another step.

'There's blood on the floor, red trails, as though
someone slaughtered pigs and dragged their
bleeding carcasses across the tiles. An arc of blood
has splashed across the kitchen window, rivulets are
steaming down, forming lines, contrasting with the
cascading rain outside.

'The oilcloth on the table is tacky, with a red

handprint like a drawing stamped at its edge. My boots are sticking, every movement sounds like the tearing of toffee paper. I stumble forward, my stomach contracting, bowels loosening and head spinning. I try to make sense of what I see.

*

'Bloody footprints show the track of the struggle. The first blow must have been struck at the kitchen sink, where Maria was peeling vegetables. Carrots and potatoes sit in pink water. I see where she stumbled backward towards the table. The bloody handprint is hers: she had leaned on the table for support. The footprints track from the kitchen, through the closed scullery door. I follow them, searching for my sister, terrified of what Ma has done to her.

'The scullery is dark. The shelves are spotless; Maria cleaned them yesterday. I see drops of blood on the stone floor — so few, compared to the kitchen. I follow their track to a dark corner, and feel a scream rise again. She's slumped there, a figure against the wall in a foetal huddle, but I can't make out the features. I take a step closer, then another and I see the apron, the hair.

'Ma is dead, the green handle of the potato peeler protruding from her eye. A single line of blood snakes from the wound, oozing down and around her nose, curving about her cheek and onto her top lip, and dripping into her open mouth. I recoil at the macabre image of my dead mother, drinking her own blood. Ma is dead — Maria killed her.

'The scream comes, growing louder and louder until all the world is a scream. I became the scream; it emptied me out into the darkness until it left nothing of the boy.'

*

I remember the rest on my own — not straightaway, but during the following hours, with Cathryn holding me tight. She kisses me, then. And later I kiss her back.

Cathryn knew, she'd known from the start that Maria had killed our mother. Maria wanted me to remember what she had done and to forgive her.

'She couldn't bear to lose you twice,' Cathryn whispers in my ear, as she holds me.

'She thought you'd blame her, hate her.'

The remaining memories came in fragments at first. Then, in a flood: Maria's hands guiding me away, laying me down on the couch, her hair falling over my facer.

"Don't hold on to this, Danny," she said. "Let it go, or it will ruin your life."

But I didn't let it go. The memory remained, festering in a deep part of me, like a cancer.

*

'When I awoke on the sofa, Da was clinging onto me. I was shaking, ripping, heaving sobs and Da was holding me tight.

"You're all right, Danny, you're ok."

'I pointed through the kitchen; the scullery door was once again closed.

"I know," Da said. "I'll take care of it. It'll be ok, I swear."

'He rocked me. I was fourteen years old, and my Da rocked me as though I was a child.

'He left me on the couch. I slept or dozed, overwhelmed by emotions. I woke to the sound of scrubbing and the forward and backward slap of a mop on linoleum. The boiler was blazing, steam rising into the already humid air.

'I tried to stand but Da pushed me back, gently. "Stay put, Danny."

'Later, Da carried me to my bed, cradling me, telling me to sleep. But I lay awake all night listening to the sounds of him working in the barn and the winch chains rattling. I realised that everything had changed. And I watched the play of shadows and the glow of orange reflecting from the blaze of the straw boiler.

'He'd made it too hot,' I thought. 'He'll destroy the mash.'

'But Da wanted the boiler hot, hot as hell, and he wasn't cooking mash for the pigs.

'Da came back before sunrise. He'd cleaned everything, removed all trace of the struggle and slaughter. And when he had done everything, he stripped off his working clothes and put them into a used potato sack before putting on a suit. Da's neatness and sense of order allowed him to destroy all traces of his wife's death and his daughter's disappearance.'

*

'Still later, he made toast and tea, and we ate in the front room on the couch, plates balanced on our knees and mugs steaming on the floor.

"Maria and your Ma left here together," Da said.

'I made to contradict him, but he held my hand

215

and squeezed.

'They took clothes with them and money, and we don't know where they went.'

'He looked at me. "Do you understand, Daniel?" I nodded; I knew this was important because he only ever called me by my full name when I was in trouble.

"Nothing else," he warned. 'Just that, they left together, they took clothes and money, and we don't know where they went." He looked at me, pain etched into his face.

"Now tell me, Danny, I want to hear you saying it."

'He made me repeat the words ten times, then ten times more.

"I'll go to the Guarda and report them missing."

'I reached out for him, not wanting to be on my own, and he pulled me to him, hugging me, crushing me against him.

"I'm sorry, Danny, for everything you've seen, and all she did to you, but it's over now, I swear."

'He stood up then and took a deep breath to steady himself. He'd created a truth so simple and so believable that no one would ever question it.

Ma was an alcoholic, she abused her children, and they — the people of the village — knew. And they believed Maria was simple-minded. No one would investigate, no one would care, except us.

"If anyone comes while I am away, try to hide," he ordered. "And, if you can't hide, you remember what to say. I trust you, Dan."

'He smiled, sad but real. He looks about the house, a small, neat man, his eyes forlorn, and then he left and I was alone.'

*

'Ma and Maria left today, they took clothes and money, I don't know where they went.'

I repeated the words so many times that they became the truth.

A new beginning

'Danni!'

The call is long and drawn out, the voice familiar, containing echoes of us all — of Da, me, even of Ma. I turn towards Maria, but it's not me she is calling.

A child runs through the long grass, her hair dark, her face impish, laughing. I watch my niece run to her mother.

Behind us, the sound of the machines is a low, steady rumble. Maria swings Danni around, they laugh, and she turns towards me, holding her hand out. I take it, and we walk back through the yard.

'Be careful, Danni,' Maria whispers as we stand on the rubble where the feather-house had been.

Behind us were the barn and the machine shed, and in front of us the house. The builders will demolish it today, and in a week nothing will remain. Soon new houses will replace the lank grass.

'What would Da think?' I ask.

'He hated it; he'd be glad to see it all gone,' Maria answers. 'He loved us, you know.'

I nod.

'It wasn't only us she abused,' she says.

I nod again, knowing that he loved her.

'It took all of us to kill her.' Maria is looking at me, her eyes intent.

'All except me.'

She laughs. There's no sign of the damage in her open, happy face. .

'It was you banging the door that distracted her, Danny. If not for you, it would have been me dead, not her.'

I think about this revelation, and the part I played in my mother's death and find it doesn't displease me.

*

We talked all the way from the city to the village. I learn about Maria's life, the man she loves, the birth of Daniella, her fear that I would not forgive her.

I would give much to say the weight shifted, and that the blackness disappeared, but that will take time. We wait for the machines to come. We don't own the house or the farm anymore; Maria organised the sale, which would bring us enough money, she says, to help both of us make a fresh start — a grim inheritance.

*

Before I left the studio to meet Maria, I called Cathryn to thank her for everything.

'You have my number,' she'd said. 'Call me if you need anything.'

'What if I need nothing, but want to call you, anyway?'

She laughed. 'I'd like that, Dan.'

*

The machine trundles into the yard; the barn vibrates, and I see the chain and the blocks; I wonder suddenly whatever happened to those last six pigs, but it's not important.

The machine moves over the rubble of the feather-house and rolls to a stop, a clawed blade extends and then drops.

I turn towards the Lady in the Glass and I salute her, then the blade descends and sweeps her away.